INTO THE WOODS

The Utes saw Nate the moment he broke from cover. Shouts, then arrows flew all around him. He ran a zigzag course to make it harder for the Utes to hit him. A glance showed all five Utes had darted from concealment and were in hot pursuit.

A speeding shaft caught Nate high on the right shoulder and spun him completely around. Somehow he retained his balance and his momentum carried him forward into the trees. He collided with a trunk, bounced off, and stood still, fighting off the shock that threatened to numb his mind and seal his doom.

Nate sprinted for all he was worth, racing deeper and deeper into the forest. The harder his legs pumped, the faster he bled, and he worried about weakening from the loss of blood. It was a risk he had to take. He dared not slow down until he lost the warriors. If he lost them....

The *Wilderness* series published by *Leisure Books:*

Mountain
Manhunt

David Thompson

LEISURE BOOKS   NEW YORK CITY

To Lisa and Vail Marie Kendall—
the apples of Scott's eye.

A LEISURE BOOK®

February 1993

Published by

Dorchester Publishing Co., Inc.
276 Fifth Avenue
New York, NY 10001

Chapter One

Nathaniel King was warily descending a gradual slope when he heard a low, wavering moan from somewhere below him. All around him branches were being rustled and bent by strong northwesterly gusts, so he assumed the sound he heard was nothing more than the wind howling among the pines that covered the lower half of the mountain. When the sound was repeated, though, he reined up and cocked his head, listening intently. There had been an odd quality about the noise, and a free trapper abroad in hostile Indian territory could ill afford to ignore any strange sounds. When the moan was repeated for the third time, he became certain it was a human voice and not the wind.

Squaring his broad shoulders, Nate hefted his Hawken rifle and guided his Palouse in the direction the moan came from. The wind whipped the fringe on his buckskins and stirred his shoulder-length black hair and beard. If he

5

David Thompson

read the signs right, a storm was brewing. By nightfall it would strike.

Since he was in the heart of Ute country and the Utes had long been after his hair, he checked his many weapons as he advanced. Wedged under his wide brown leather belt, one on either side of the large buckle, were two flintlocks. On his left hip hung a butcher knife, on his right a tomahawk. Crisscrossing his broad chest was a powder horn and an ammo pouch. He was ready for trouble should it come, but he preferred to avoid fighting the Utes if he could.

Near the bottom he spied a clearing, and at its center the smoldering remains of a campfire. Halting, he surveyed the valley beyond, then focused once more on the clearing. There was no sign of anyone. If the Utes had been there, they must be gone. But who, then, had moaned?

Yet another pitiable wail drew his attention to a tall fir bordering the east side of the clearing. For a few seconds he saw nothing except deep shadows. Then, with a start, he realized there was a naked man hanging upside down from a rope. This man, who was facing the other way, dangled a good 15 feet above the ground.

Nate looked around again for others but saw no one. Half-convinced the man was alone, he touched his thumb to the hammer of his rifle and slowly advanced until he reached the edge of the clearing. Fresh tracks told him part of the story. There had been Indians here, seven or eight of them, and not long ago. After stringing up their victim they had ridden off to the southwest.

Turning to the right, Nate rode around the clearing until he could see the man's face. Then he stopped. It was a white man, 40 or so, lean of build but muscular, his eyes closed, his arms dangling limply, blood dripping from a nasty gash on his forehead. Otherwise he appeared unhurt. "Hello," Nate ventured softly.

The man's eyes snapped open and he looked right and left until he spotted Nate. He blinked, licked his thin lips, and said, "You ain't no damn Ute."

"Luckily for you. I'm surprised they left you alive. Usually they're not so charitable." Nate moved closer while constantly scouring the vegetation, not relaxing his guard for an instant.

"They wanted this coon to hang here for a spell while they went off to tend to some business. They're fixin' to come back and finish the job shortly."

"They told you this?"

"I overhead 'em jawin'. Couldn't make out every word but I know a little of their tongue." The man gingerly touched his brow. "After one of the bastards walloped me I played possum. I was hopin' they'd get careless and give me a chance to escape, but they stripped me down and strung me up here with my own rope." He sadly shook his head. "Hell of a note."

"I'll climb that tree and cut you down."

"No need, friend. Just toss me your pigsticker and I'll take care of it."

Nate rode directly under the limb from which the man hung, then introduced himself as he drew his knife.

"I'm Solomon Cain," the man revealed, and added with a lopsided grin. "My folks were real Biblical when it came to namin' their young'uns."

"Here," Nate said, tossing his knife, hilt first, straight up. With a jab of his heels he moved the Palouse to one side in case Cain should miss and the knife should fall back down, but Cain deftly caught it by the dull side of the blade.

"I admire a man who knows how to keep his knives sharp," Cain commented after lightly pressing his thumb to the keen edge. "Scalped many Injuns with this?"

"A few," Nate admitted, displeased by the question. Scalping was not a practice he believed in or practiced regularly, even if he was an adopted Shoshone.

"I never have," Cain said, and began to slowly ease his torso upward. "Too savage for my tastes."

Nate's estimation of the man rose a notch. He kept one eye on Cain and the other on the valley on the chance the Utes might return ahead of schedule.

Cain gritted his teeth and raised his hands level with his knees. His face turned beet red, his stomach muscles quivered violently, and suddenly, with a gasp, he sank back down again. "Damned noggin'," he muttered. "Poundin' worse than a cannon."

"Sure you don't need my help?"

"No, thanks. I got myself into this fix, I'll get myself out," Cain replied. Again clamping his teeth together, he tilted his head to gaze at his bound ankles, then surged upward with all the strength he could muster. This time his left hand touched his left ankle before the tremendous strain and the irresistible pull of gravity caused him to fall back. "Damn. Damn. Damn," he mumbled. "If I ever get my hands on Flying Hawk, I'm goin' to skin him alive."

"You *know* the Ute who did this to you?"

"Sort of."

"How do you 'sort of' know someone?"

"He's sort of my brother-in-law since I sort of stole his sister for my wife," Cain said. "Ever since then he's had it in for me."

"I can't imagine why," Nate said dryly, amazed by the disclosure. So far as he knew, no other white man had ever taken a Ute woman for his wife simply because the Utes either drove off or killed any whites they found in their territory. While not as bloodthirsty as the widely feared Blackfeet, the Utes were a proud, independent tribe who fiercely prevented any attempts by outsiders to penetrate their domain, and they had been doing this for more years than anyone could remember. During the last century, when the Spanish were spreading their dominion over the southwest and often venturing into the rugged Rockies, the Utes had repeatedly raided Spanish settlements, driving off large numbers of horses in the process. There were some old-timers who claimed the Utes had been among the very first Indians to own the animals that wound up totally changing the Indian way of life, at least for those tribes dependent on the buffalo for their existence.

Cain had ignored the sarcasm. Tensing his body, he abruptly surged upward and succeeded in grabbing hold of his left ankle. Then, holding fast, he sawed at the knots, parting strand after strand.

"You'd better . . ." Nate began, about to warn Cain to grab onto the length of rope secured to the tree limb, but before he could complete his sentence the loops around Cain's ankles parted and the man plummeted earthward.

Cain tried to flip in midair so he would land on his feet, but he was only halfway around when he struck, hitting hard on his buttocks and rolling end over end until he slammed into the base of a tree.

Quickly sliding off his gelding, Nate ran over. "Solomon? How badly are you hurt?"

"I'm fine," Cain said, grunting as he uncoiled and stood. There was a dark circle on his left shoulder and pine needles were caked to his skin. "Just bruised, is all." He leaned against the tree and frowned. "It hasn't been a good day."

"So I gather," Nate responded, gauging the other's size. "I have a spare pair of leggins you're welcome to use if you want. They'll be a little big on you but we can tie them up with some rope." He spotted his knife on the ground and retrieved it.

"I don't want to be a bother."

"You'd rather go around naked?"

9

"I reckon I wouldn't," Cain conceded. He stared out over the verdant valley. "And you'd best hurry. I know my brain's been addled by the fall, but I swear that's a dust cloud I see yonder."

A glance confirmed there was a party of riders descending a barren hill to the southwest. They were better than half a mile off, yet there was no mistaking the way some of them were energetically using quirts on their mounts and the fact that a few of the riders weren't wearing shirts.

"The Utes," Nate said, and dashed to his horse. It took but a moment to open the proper parfleche and remove his extra leggins, which he immediately carried to his new companion.

"The devils are comin' back sooner than I figured," Cain commented as he stuck first his right leg, then his left into the buckskin britches. "I knew they would! Nothin' is going the way it should lately." Swiftly he pulled the leggins all the way up and bunched the waistband in his right fist. "Flying Hawk probably couldn't wait to roast me alive."

"Can you ride?" Nate asked.

"If I can't I'll sprout wings."

"Climb on behind me," Nate directed as he stepped to the Palouse and swung up. "Pegasus can bear both of us for quite a spell. With luck, we'll lose those Utes."

"Pegasus?" Cain repeated. "You gave your horse a name?"

"Why shouldn't I?"

"No reason. But I make it a practice never to give a name to something I might have to eat one day."

Nate gave the Palouse a pat, then lowered his right arm. "I'd never eat this horse. It was a gift from the Nez Percé, and I've never known a finer animal anywhere."

"A man who is hungry enough will eat anything," Cain asserted, taking hold of Nate's hand. "I should

10

know. I got myself lost once, ran out of food, couldn't find so much as a chipmunk to shoot, and I wound up eating some bugs I found under a log."

The mere thought of swallowing a mouthful of crunchy insects made Nate's stomach churn. He hauled Cain up behind him, then clucked Pegasus into a trot, bearing to the northeast, out across the valley. There were plenty of trees and thickets to afford cover, enabling him to cross to a stark mountain on the other side without being seen by the Utes. Angling upward, he climbed high enough to clearly view their back trail, and beheld a sight that made his blood race. A quarter of a mile off were the seven Utes, coming on fast. "One of them must be a good tracker," he commented.

"Flying Hawk is. His sister claims he can track an ant over solid rock."

"Let's hope she's mistaken," Nate said. "Hang on!"

They were galloping to beat the wind when they reached the bottom and cut sharply to the right. Nate wisely hugged the mountain until a curve hid most of the valley from sight. Then he veered to the right to scale a ridge. In a stand of aspens at the top he drew rein and twisted in the saddle. "Sit tight while I'll discourage them."

Cain glanced at the Hawken. "I'd rather keep ridin' if it's all the same to you."

"If I kill one or two the rest might give up."

"You said your horse can outrun them."

"For a while. But why run Pegasus into the ground when a few shots might end this right here and now?" Nate said.

"You might hit Flying Hawk."

"So?"

"So his sister would never forgive me."

Annoyed and baffled, Nate reluctantly resumed their flight. He didn't know what to make of Cain. One minute the man wanted to kill Flying Hawk. The next he wanted to spare the Ute from harm. Any sane man would want Flying Hawk dead, particularly if the Ute was after Cain's scalp as Cain contended. Then there was this business of the sister. Why was Cain so concerned about the feelings of a woman who must despise him terribly for spiriting her away from her people? None of it made any sense to him, and he speculated on whether or not Solomon Cain might be touched in the head.

It wasn't a common condition, but it wasn't all that rare either. Quite a few trappers had been overwhelmed by the devastating hardships of life in the Rockies and succumbed to the secret terrors that fester in men's souls. He remembered one trapper in particular who had sunk to the depths of depravity, going so far as to become a cannibal when during the middle of an especially severe winter the man and his Flathead wife ran out of food and they were unable to hunt because of snow over ten feet deep outside their isolated cabin. The trapper had done the only thing he could to survive, and forever after he had borne the mental scars. Crazy George, they'd all called him. Not until much later did the other members of the trapping fraternity learn why he had gone over the edge.

Such gruesome thoughts disturbed Nate greatly. He didn't like the notion of riding with someone who might see fit to yank out his own knife and slit his throat at any moment. Then he reminded himself that he had no proof that Cain was crazy. And there might well be a perfectly logical explanation for Cain's behavior. Still, he rode with his elbows tucked close to his body so that Cain couldn't grab for his knife or tomahawk without him being aware of it.

For half an hour he pushed Pegasus as hard as he dared, deliberately sticking to the roughest terrain and the hardest ground. When he saw rocky tracts, he crossed them. When he came to a narrow stream he entered it and rode downstream for a mile before riding out onto the bank. Always he stayed shy of the skyline. During his time with the Shoshones he had learned to ride as they did, and he now employed every trick they had taught him.

Presently he climbed a ridge for a bird's-eye panoramic view of the countryside. He was elated to discover there was no sign of the Utes. Yet, anyway. "Maybe we've lost them," he mentioned hopefully.

"I wouldn't count on it," Cain said. "They want Smoky Woman back in the worst way. But I'll never let 'em get her." He paused. "I love her, King, with all my heart."

Nate was tempted to ask if the Ute woman felt the same about Cain, but he decided not to. One of the first lessons a trapper learned was to never, ever meddle in the personal affairs of others. Then too, he knew how he would feel if anyone had the audacity to question his love for his own wife, Winona, a lovely Shoshone.

"We should keep goin'," Cain advised. "Once I know for sure we've given 'em the slip, I'll guide you to where Smoky Woman and I are livin'. It's not all that far. She'll be worried sick if I don't make it back soon."

"You mean to say you haven't moved as far from her people as you can?"

"We figure on stayin' right where we're at come hell or high water. Why?"

"Oh, no reason," Nate said, heading down the opposite side of the ridge. "I just thought it might be a little dangerous staying around here with the Utes after your hide and all. Why not move somewhere else, somewhere safer? Thirty miles to the north is about the limit of their territory. Go there and the Utes might never find you."

Cain appeared shocked by the suggestion. "I couldn't do that to Smoky Woman. She was born in this area. She loves it here."

"Is staying worth you life?"

"I'd sacrifice anything to make her happy," Cain said. "I don't suppose you can understand this, but my life without her would have no meanin'. So everything I do, I do for her."

Nate did understand the man's tender sentiments, but he labeled the sacrifice Cain was making as extremely foolish. If Smoky Woman cared a lick for Cain, she'd agree to go off somewhere, go off *anywhere*, just so the two of them were out of harm's way.

"Do you have a wife, King?"

"Yes," Nate answered, and told Cain about Winona.

"And I bet there isn't a blamed thing under the sun you wouldn't do for her," Cain said. "True love always works that way."

Pondering those words, Nate rode at a canter across a grassy meadow, pausing momentarily once to check the ridge they had just traversed. Then he plunged into dense woods, and winced when the tip of a branch nicked his cheek. More vigilant now, he weaved among the count- less trunks until they came to a series of rolling hills. The Utes had still not appeared, and he was becoming increasingly confident he'd given them the slip.

A game trail frequently used by elk and black-tailed deer enabled him to pick up the pace. Once among the hills they stumbled on a spring, and Nate promptly reined up. He let Cain get down, then dismounted and held the reins while Pegasus greedily drank.

"What matters most in life to you, King?" Cain unex- pectedly inquired.

"Call me Nate. And I'd have to say it's my family."

"Are you doin' a good job of providin' for them?"

"The best I can. We get by."

"Have you ever thought about doin' more than just gettin' by? Ever thought of being able to give them everything they could possibly want?"

14

Nate was puzzled by the line of questioning. Sinking to one knee, he splashed a handful of cool water on his cheeks and neck, then said, "There isn't a husband and father alive who doesn't have such dreams. But we have to be realistic. The fur companies aren't paying as much for prime beaver pelts as they once were. I'm happy if I can just put some money away for the future every now and then."

"You'd like to do better, though, wouldn't you?"

"Who wouldn't?" Nate retorted. "What are you getting at?"

"I was curious where you stood, is all."

Nothing else was said until after they had been riding again for over ten minutes. Cain tapped Nate on the shoulder and commented, "I owe you for pullin' my fat out of the fire back there. If you hadn't come along when you did, those devils would be torturin' me right about now."

"I did what any man would do."

"Maybe so. But the fact is you did it for me. Makes me beholden to you and I always make good on my debts." Cain placed his left hand on his hip and smugly surveyed the verdant hills. "One of these days I'm goin' to be the richest son of a gun who ever lived and I'll be able to pay you back with interest. Mark my words."

"Do you aim to do like Jed Smith did and bring in almost seven hundred pelts in a single year?"

Cain snorted. "When I talk about gettin' rich I'm not thinkin' of beaver. The only ones who make a lot of money off the trappin' trade are the owners of the fur companies. No, I have something else in mind."

Suddenly Nate detected movement in spruce trees off to the left perhaps 40 yards. Tensing, he slowed and held the Hawken in both hands while probing among the lower boughs. A vague shape materialized, a large black shape that moments later lumbered into the open. It was a bear, but not the most dreaded of all Rocky Mountain animals, not a savage grizzly. This was a full-grown black bear making its daily rounds. One look at them was enough to compel it to flee, and Nate listened to the crashing of its heavy bulk through the underbrush until the sounds became faint and faded.

Further on he saw a solitary brazen buck watching them from a nearby hilltop. Had the Utes not been on their trail he would have shot the buck for supper. As it was, his stomach growled and his mouth watered when he imagined biting into a thick slab of roast venison.

"Another mile or so should do 'er," Cain mentioned. "I guess I was wrong. You did give those Utes the shake."

"We were lucky," Nate said.

"No, you're good," Cain countered. "You're a handy man to have around in a pinch. I bet you've tangled with Injuns before."

"Once or twice."

"You even dress a lot like they do. If a man didn't know better, he might mistake *you* for an Injun."

"In a sense I am."

"How's that?"

Nate explained about being adopted by the Shoshones after his marriage to Winona, and how he was rearing his son to appreciate the customs and cultures of whites and Shoshones alike. He concluded with; "They both have a lot of good to them, but most folks, Indians and whites, are so busy criticizing what they don't understand in one another that they never see the good parts. They can't see the forest for the trees."

"Never thought of it quite that way before," Cain said. "You must exercise your brain muscles a lot."

"My wife would disagree."

Cain laughed and clapped Nate on the back. "Smoky Woman is the same way sometimes. I swear, women must be the most contrary critters in all of creation. I doubt I'd ever understand them if I lived to be a hundred."

"How's your head holding up?" Nate asked.

Before Cain could answer the rarefied mountain air was rent by the pounding rhythm of driving hoofs, and around the base of a hill up ahead swept the band of Utes, who broke into frenzied whoops of raging anticipation the instant they laid eyes on their quarry.

Chapter Two

Uttering an oath, Nate wheeled Pegasus and fled. All his efforts to lose the warriors had been in vain, merely so much wasted time. There must, he reasoned, be a shortcut through the hills known only to the Utes, or else the band had ridden like mad and circled around to get out in front of them. Now the warriors were less than two hundred yards distant, and once the gap was narrowed to half that distance the Utes would use their bows.

"Damn their bones!" Cain cried.

Nate was doing some fast thinking. He couldn't hope to outrun the band, not with Pegasus so tired. His only recourse was to find a convenient spot to make a stand and to do it quickly. But where? There was plenty of forest to hide in, but he wanted a spot where the Utes would have a hard time getting at the two of them. Moments later he saw a bunch of boulders halfway up a hill on his right, and without hesitation he took the slope on the fly, shouting, "Hang on tight!"

Cain's arms encircled his waist.

The whoops reached a crescendo when the Utes realized his intent.

Pegasus was almost to the boulders when the first arrow streaked out of the blue and smacked into the earth within a yard of the gelding's neck. A second shaft missed by even less. A third struck a boulder to one side of them. Then they were behind another boulder the size of a Shoshoni lodge, one of five of similar size forming a crude natural fortification, and they could hear more arrows cracking against the impenetrable stone surfaces.

Nate was off the Palouse and at a crack between two of the boulders before Solomon Cain began to lift his leg to climb down. The seven Utes were charging up the slope, spreading out as they did, all with bows in their hands and firing as rapidly as they could nock shafts to their bowstrings. Clearly they were counting on overwhelming Nate and Cain by sheer force of numbers.

Nate had other ideas. He pressed the Hawken to his right shoulder, cocked the hammer, and took a quick bead on the foremost Ute. Barely had the sight settled on the warrior's brawny upper chest than Nate squeezed off the shot. The ball flew true and the Ute toppled in a whirl of arms and legs.

Darting to the left, to the end of the boulders, Nate drew a flintlock and had it cocked and leveled by the time he stopped to aim at a second Ute. A buzzing shaft smacked into the earth at his feet. Another nipped on his sleeve. Concentrating on the Ute, he fired, then jumped to safety as the warrior crashed to the ground.

The charge was broken. Breaking to the right and the left, the surviving warriors made for the nearest cover, some vaulting from their mounts before the animals stopped moving. In seconds there was no sign of a single Ute, they were so well hidden.

Nate wedged the spent pistol under his belt and began reloading the Hawken, first putting the butt between his feet, then pouring the proper amount of black powder into his palm, measuring by sight. Next he hastily fed the powder from his palm down the muzzle. Swiftly wrapping a ball in a patch, he pushed both into the muzzle with his thumb, then used the ramrod to shove them down on top of the powder. All the while the slope below was eerily quiet. As he replaced the ramrod in its housing he glanced at Pegasus, and was shocked to see Solomon Cain still on the horse, bent forward over the saddle. "Were you hit?" he asked.

"No. It's my head," Cain answered. "I can barely think straight. That wallop must have rattled me worse than I figured."

"Get off and lie down," Nate directed, stepping forward. He drew the pistol he hadn't fired yet. "Here. Hold onto this. They might try to rush us again."

"Thank you," Cain said, taking hold of the flintlock by the barrel instead of the butt end. "And I want to also thank you for the loan of your horse."

Nate, already starting to turn away, stopped and glanced up. "My horse?" he said, and too late saw an object sweeping at his head. Instinctively he tried to duck but the blow connected, slamming him backwards, stunning him. His vision swam and he fell to his knees. He heard Pegasus heading up the slope and bellowed, *"No!"* Solomon Cain paid no heed. It took only five or six seconds for Nate's vision to return to normal, yet by then the gelding was a dozen yards off and gaining ground with each stride.

From scattered points below came yells of surprise, and several arrows chased the Palouse but lost the race.

Without thinking Nate whipped the Hawken up and sighted on Cain's back midway between the shoulder blades. All he had to do was pull back the hammer, then squeeze off the shot. Yet he hesitated. Shooting a man in the back went against his grain. In his estimation it was the same as cold-blooded murder, and while he had killed many times to save his life or the lives of those dear to him, he took consolation in the fact he wasn't a wanton murderer.

His hesitation didn't last, however. Cain was stealing his horse, leaving him afoot, stranding him in the middle of nowhere with a band of bloodthirsty Utes about to close in. Now was not the time for scruples, he reflected, and his trigger finger tightened.

Cain cut into a stand of trees and disappeared.

Furious, Nate relaxed his finger and moved closer to the boulders. He was hoping to see Pegasus emerge from the evergreens, riderless, and trot back to him. The gelding had a passionate dislike for being ridden by anyone else. If a stranger tried to climb up, the Palouse would shy away, kick or buck. Not this time, though. Apparently, since Cain had already been on Pegasus, had in fact ridden double a considerable distance with Nate, Pegasus had grown accustomed to Cain's presence and didn't mind Cain being in the saddle.

A shrill whistle alerted Nate to a more urgent problem.

He crouched and peered through a crack. Some of the Utes were stealthily working their way toward the boulders. He glimpsed two of them, fleeting shadows impossible to shoot. Soon they would be on him.

Nate scowled in anger at the turn of events, girded his legs, and sprinted to the left, going from boulder to boulder until he was in the clear and racing madly for fir trees a score of yards off. The Utes saw him the moment he broke from cover. Shouts broke out, arrows flew all around him. He ran a zigzag course to make it harder for the Utes to hit him. A glance showed all five Utes had darted from concealment and were in hot pursuit. Two of the three abruptly realized they would fare better on horseback and ran for their horses, which had strayed toward the bottom of the slope. He had to reach the trees before they mounted and came after him or his life was forfeit.

His feet fairly flew over the ground. He tried not to think of what would happen should he trip. The Utes were howling, certain they would soon have him in their clutches. The tree line drew closer. And closer. Now he could see the individual leaves and the knots on the trunks. Just a few more feet and he would be there!

A speeding shaft caught him high on the right shoulder and spun him completely around. Somehow he retained his balance and his momentum carried him forward into the trees. He collided with a trunk, bounced off, and stood still, fighting off the shock that threatened to numb his mind and seal his doom.

Waves of agony washed over him, eclipsing the shock, restoring his senses. The bloody point of the slender arrow jutted several inches out from his throbbing shoulder and he could see red drops spattering onto his shirt. His hand still held the Hawken, but his fingers were beginning to feel numb so he reached across and took the rifle in his left hand. Then he ran.

The fleetest Utes were within 15 yards of the tree line.

He sprinted for all he was worth, racing deeper and deeper into the forest. The harder his legs pumped, the faster he bled, and he worried about weakening from the loss of blood. It was a risk he had to take. He dared not slow down until he lost the warriors. If he lost them.

At length his legs began to tire. A look back showed that he had temporarily outdistanced the Utes, who must have lost sight of him and would now be tracking him down. He slowed, then slanted to the right, heading up the slope where he might find a spot where he could try and hold the Utes off. If a fight came he wanted the advantage of the high ground.

Eventually the trees gave way to a rocky stretch of slope. There he exercised extreme care, jumping from stone to stone wherever possible to leave as few tracks as possible. He came to a place where erosion had worn out a shallow gully and into this he sank, lying on his left side with the Hawken in front of him.

Now he could catch his breath and take stock. The wound had stopped bleeding but hurt abominably. He knew the arrow must come out, and the sooner the better. Gripping the shaft below the point, he clamped his front teeth together, bunched his muscles, and exerted all the pressure he could. The shaft trembled, aggravating the torment. He could feel sweat covering his forehead. The veins on his neck were standing out. And suddenly the arrow broke with a loud snap.

Nate tossed the bloody tip from him in disgust, then twisted and tried to get a grip on the part of the shaft protruding from his back. His slick palm slipped twice, so he wiped it clean on his leggins and tried again. This time he succeeded in taking hold, but strain as he might he did no more than move the shaft a fraction of an inch. How was he ever going to get it out?

Letting go, he sank down, his brow in the dirt, and took deep breaths. He was in the fix of his life. Sooner or later the Utes would track him to the gully. Should he stay and fight or keep running?

Shouts broke out below. Propping himself on his elbow, he saw a pair of Utes on horseback near the cluster of boulders where he had made his stand. They were yelling and pointing at the crest of the hill. Shifting, he discovered the reason. Solomon Cain had reached the top and stopped to gaze down. The Utes took off after him.

So now there were three to contend with, Nate reflected. Sinking back, he accidentally bumped the arrow against the side of the gully and grimaced at the fresh pain that engulfed him. His right arm tingled and nausea gnawed at him.

He had to keep climbing. Grabbing the Hawken, he rose awkwardly and scanned the slope. Cain had vanished and the two Utes were halfway to the crest. Nothing moved in the forest, which meant little. The three remaining Utes might already know where he was hiding and be waiting for him to show himself.

Nate stepped out of the gully, hunched over, and continued climbing. He felt sluggish and had extreme difficulty concentrating. Fearful he might collapse and pass out, he hurried as best he was able. Constantly he checked the forest below, and also noted the progress of the two Utes going after Cain, both of whom soon went over the top. He saw them go with mixed feelings. On the one hand he wanted them to overtake Cain and give the bastard a dose of his own medicine, but on the other he was worried about them taking Pegasus.

He went 30 yards before his legs gave out. One second he was plodding steadily upward in grim determination. The next his face was in the dirt and he was inhaling dust. Angered by the betrayal of his own body, he rolled onto his back, then managed to sit up. Nearby was a waist-high boulder, the only cover available.

Using the stock of the Hawken as a crutch, Nate got himself behind the boulder. Sitting with his back to it, he closed his eyes and struggled with the tide of exhaustion on the verge of overwhelming him.

When would he learn? he asked himself. How long would it be before he realized he couldn't blindly trust every stranger he came across in his travels? Several times, now, his unthinking trust had jeopardized his life. He had to do as his best friend and mentor Shakespeare

McNair advised, "Be neighborly but keep your hand on your gun."

The sunlight warmed his face, making him drowsy. His eyelids fluttered as he valiantly strived to stay awake. But the ordeal proved too much for him. A black cloud seemed to consume his consciousness and he faded into oblivion.

He awoke to the sensation of small drops of moisture striking his face. Disoriented, he sat with his eyes closed, trying to recall where he was and what had happened. In a rush of memories he recalled everything just as thunder boomed in the distance.

Nate blinked and looked all around him. He was amazed to see twilight shrouded the Rocky Mountains because it meant he'd slept for hours. Miraculously, the Utes hadn't found him. More drops struck his cheeks and he stared up at the roiling clouds sweeping past overhead. The storm he had expected was almost upon him.

Lightning lanced the sky to the west, emphasizing how exposed he was to the elements. The last place he wanted to be was out in the open when the storm unleashed its full fury. Wounded and weak as he was, a thorough soaking might be all that was needed to render him helplessly ill.

Bracing his left hand on the boulder, he shoved to his feet. The Utes, evidently, were long gone since their horses were no longer to be seen. He headed for an isolated stand of trees to the east, and just reached them when the rain changed from tiny drops into great big ones and the heavens rumbled mightily.

Finding a patch of undergrowth, he dropped to his hands and knees and crawled into the brush, parting branches with his rifle so they wouldn't catch on the arrow. There, partially sheltered, he lay flat and listened to the howling wind.

He would be going nowhere for a while. Resting his chin on his left forearm, he contemplated the folly that had led him into the fix he was in. His never-ending search for beaver had taken him far from his usual haunts, where the beaver were harder to find with each passing trapping season. He needed somewhere new to trap, somewhere where the animals hadn't been depleted. And since few whites had ever ventured into Ute country, he'd figured he should be able to find an ideal locale there.

If he'd had any brains he would have listened to Winona and gone into the remote country to the northwest of their cabin, not to the southwest into Ute land. Now the harm was done, in more ways than one.

The rain was pouring down, the wind curling the saplings and shaking the branches of the taller trees. Some of the drops got through to him, but not enough to make him uncomfortable. A dank scent filled his nostrils. Drowsiness returned but he resisted an urge to sleep.

Since he was stuck there, he might as well make the best of it, he decided. Drawing his knees up under him, he lowered his forehead to the ground, then reached back with both hands and grasped the arrow. His right shoulder pulsed with exquisite anguish, which he shut from his mind. The arrow had to come out. To leave it in much longer invited infection.

Grunting, he pulled on the shaft with all of his strength. The arrow stubbornly budged a fraction of an inch but no more. Again he tried, working the shaft from side to side to loosen it, and felt fresh blood trickle down his chest. He broke out in perspiration from head to toe.

Repeatedly he pulled on the arrow, and gradually it began to slide out. After each strenuous exertion he had to rest for a few minutes. Then he had another go at it. His buckskin shirt around the entry and exit wounds was soaked with blood when, to his joy, the shaft slid free.

Exhausted again, he slumped down and stared at the bloody arrow. He hadn't thought to examine the barbed point earlier to see if it had been coated with poison, which could prove a fatal oversight. Sometimes Indians dipped the heads of their shafts in rattlesnake venom or dead animals. Contact with warm blood released the poison into the system and death was a slow, agonizing affair.

Nate put the arrow down and sat up. Beyond the thicket the storm was in full swing. Lightning lit the sky again and again. More rain was reaching him, yet so far he had avoided being drenched. He quickly collected a handful of small, dry twigs and dry weeds. Forming them into a compact pile with a depression in the middle, he leaned over the pile to further protect it from the rain, then opened his bullet pouch and took out his oval fire steel, his flint, and punk. Placing the punk in the depression, he set about producing sparks by striking the flint with slicing blows of the fire steel. Soon he had the punk burning. The tiny flames spread to the grass. By adding larger branches he got a small fire going in no time.

Now came the hard part. Replacing the steel and flint in his pouch, he removed his shirt. Then he pulled the Hawken's ramrod out and held the ramrod over the flames until the heated end practically glowed red hot. He was ready. Aligning the hot end with the exit wound in his shoulder, he bit down on a thick piece of branch, held his breath, and shoved the ramrod into the hole. Searing pain shot through him. He could smell his own burning flesh. His courage faltered and he almost released the ramrod, but didn't. The wound had to be cauterized. If the point of the arrow had been poisoned this was the only way of saving himself.

The ramrod went halfway and became stuck. Yanking it out, he once more applied the end to the fire. A job half-finished was no job at all. Shortly, the ramrod was hot enough and he stuck it into the hole. This time the task was easier and he poked the ramrod all the way through, unable to resist a shudder at the uncomfortable sensation.

Once he had the ramrod out, he sank down onto his left side, limp and weak, drained of all energy. He lay still, hearing the crackling fire and the intermittent crash of thunder. If he survived until morning, he would be out of danger. His next priority would be to regain his strength. Then what?

There could be only one answer. He was going after Solomon Cain. He would get Pegasus back. And he would insure that Cain never stole another horse from anyone else.

A cold breeze gave him gooseflesh and revived him. His fire had died. Sluggishly, he sat up, realizing the rain had stopped. The sky was silent. Craning his head, he peered through the branches and spotted twinkling stars.

He'd slept again! Yet he was far from being refreshed. Donning his shirt, he curled up into a ball, his hands between his legs for warmth, and permitted sleep to claim him once more.

When next Nate opened his eyes the sun ruled the heavens. He rose to his knees to gingerly inspect his shoulder. There was no trace of bleeding, no evidence of swelling or discoloration. Apparently the cauterization had been successful.

He checked the Hawken because he couldn't remember if he'd reloaded it or not, and found he had. The pistol, though, needed loading, so he did so before he turned and crawled from his hiding place. Squinting in the bright light, he slowly rose and adjusted his knife and his tomahawk so they hung properly.

Although he could hardly wait to pursue Cain, he knew he needed nourishment first. His jerked venison, pemmican, and the other food Winona had packed for him were all in a parfleche on Pegasus. To eat he had to find game.

Cocking the Hawken and touching the stock to his left shoulder, he hiked toward the bottom of the hill, deliberately making as much noise as he could as he went from brush patch to brush patch. When, minutes later, a rabbit bolted to the west, he was ready. Or thought he was. For he found that holding the Hawken in exactly the opposite way as he normally did and sighting along the barrel with his left eye instead of his right was an ungainly experience. He couldn't seem to get a bead on his breakfast, and was about to lower the rifle when the rabbit helped him out by stopping to stare at him. A second later a ball ripped through its brain.

Nate dashed over to the twitching animal, then scoured the hill and the surrounding countryside. If the Utes were still in the area they might have heard the shot. It would be wise to head elsewhere to cook his meal. Accordingly, he reloaded the rifle as fast as he could with his right arm being so stiff and sore, then picked up the rabbit and made for the crest.

At the top he halted in dismay on finding the barren earth a blank slate. The storm had washed out every last hoofprint. Now he had no way of tracking Cain, of reclaiming Pegasus.

Simmering with frustration, Nate hiked down into dense woodland. For over a mile he pressed on until he came to a clearing flanked by a gurgling stream. There he slaked his parched throat, then built a small fire directly under overspreading tree limbs so the branches would disperse what little smoke the fire gave off.

Gutting and skinning the rabbit was easily accomplished. He sharpened a stick, jabbed the pointed end

David Thompson

through several pieces of raw meat, and held the make-shift spit over the low flames. The tantalizing aroma the rabbit soon gave off made his mouth water in anticipation.

Presently the meat was cooked enough to suit him and he took a bite, savoring the delicious taste. Closing his eyes, he chewed slowly, knowing he might become sick if he bolted his food. While he had often enjoyed rabbit in the past, it had never ranked as one of his favorites. He much preferred deer and panther meat, especially the latter, which was the most flavorful meat in all creation according to those privileged to eat some. But this rabbit, he mused, had to be about the best meat he'd ever had.

Suddenly Nate froze. He thought he'd heard the soft pad of stealthy footfall. Gulping down his mouthful of meat, he opened his eyes and swiveled around to find a lone Ute stalking toward him with an arrow already trained on his back.

Chapter
Three

Nate King was certain he was going to die, certain he would momentarily feel the warrior's shaft tear through his torso. He'd left the Hawken propped against the nearby tree, perhaps five feet away, so near, yet not near enough to grab before the Ute let the arrow fly. But he still had a flintlock. He started to rise, his left hand falling to the pistol, when the Ute barked a single word. The warrior now had the arrow aimed at his face and was advancing swiftly. There was no way the man could miss at such close range, even if Nate tried to leap aside.

The Ute spoke a string of words and motioned with the bow, indicating Nate should lift his hand away from the pistol.

Nate hesitated. Evidently the Ute intended to take him alive, which might buy him time to turn the tables. One thing was for sure; he'd rather chance being able to catch the warrior unawares later than die right then and there.

Reluctantly he raised his hands to shoulder height.

The Ute halted eight feet off and again addressed him.

"I don't savvy," Nate said in English. Then, in Shoshone, "I do not understand."

By the warrior's expression it was obvious he had no idea what Nate had said. The Ute gestured with the bow and bobbed it up and down.

At first Nate failed to comprehend. Then the man made a jabbing motion at his waist, and the meaning became all too clear. He was being instructed to dispose of the flintlock and his other weapons. Using two fingers and exaggerated, slow movements so the Ute could see he was not about to do anything rash, Nate pulled the pistol out and gently placed it on the ground. He did likewise with his butcher knife and the tomahawk, then stepped back when the Ute indicated he should do so, and kept on stepping until the Ute signified he should stop.

The warrior appeared to relax slightly.

Nate held himself perfectly still and waited for the Ute to make the next move. He expected the warrior to either give a yell to attract the rest of the band or else force him to turn and kneel so the Ute could bind him, although what the man would use he had no idea since the only other article the warrior had was a knife. To his amazement, the man abruptly lowered the bow to the ground and straightened with his palms held outward to show he had peaceful intention.

"Where is he?" the Ute then inquired, using sign language. "If you can talk with your hands, tell me."

So surprised was Nate that he simply stood there until the warrior repeated the question. Collecting his wits, Nate finally signed in response, "Who do you mean?"

"The white devil whose tongue knows no truth," the Ute elaborated.

"Solomon Cain," Nate muttered in English. His hands flowed in flawless sign. "If I knew where he was I would cut out his tongue and feed it to coyotes."

Now it was the warrior's turn to seem dumbfounded. "He is not your friend?"

"No."

"But you cut him down and rode off with him."

"That was my mistake. If I had known he would try to split my skull and steal my horse I never would have helped the dog," Nate signed, and was mystified when the Ute's features hardened.

"He does it to his own people too. Truly he is a man without honor."

"Would you care to explain?"

The Ute's hands moved. "I am Flying Hawk," he began.

"You are the brother of the woman the dog took as his wife," Nate interrupted, and tensed when the Ute suddenly rushed toward him. He thought the man was about to attack, but the warrior halted a yard away.

"You saw her? You saw Smoky Woman?"

"No. He told me about her."

"What did he tell you?"

"That he stole her and made her his wife, and that you have been after him ever since."

Flying Hawk had the look of a man who wanted to kill something. Or someone. "False Tongue has told the truth for once. My sister was out with other women gathering berries when he took her against her will. All the men in our village went after them but he was too clever for us. That was when I took a vow to find him and save Smoky Woman no matter how long it takes. Some of my friends agreed to go with me. We have been hunting him for a long time."

"And you finally found him," Nate signed when the warrior stopped and bowed his head.

"Yes. We took him by surprise and hung him from a tree while we decided what to do with him. Some of my friends wanted to cut off his fingers and gouge out his eyes unless he told us where Smoky Woman was. I was afraid he would die before he told us and then we would never find her. He heard us talking. He claimed she was at his camp, over the next hill. So we rode off to see, leaving him there since we expected to quickly return."

Nate didn't need to hear the rest. That was when he had happened along and set Cain free, ruining any hope Flying Hawk had of rescuing his sister. "I am sorry," he signed. "Had I known I never would have helped him."

Flying Hawk studied Nate for a moment. "I do not blame you, white man. False Tongue is as clever as a fox."

"False Tongue? Is that the name your people have given him?"

"It is the name *I* gave him after he lied to me."

"How long has he had your sister?"

"Four moons."

Four months! Nate could well imagine the emotional misery the warrior must have gone through since the abduction. "How old is your sister?"

There was a haunted aspect to the Ute's dark eyes when he answered. "She has lived sixteen winters."

Nate's initial reaction was to think, "She's so young." Then he reminded himself that Indian maidens often married at that age or even younger. Sometimes the marriages were forced on them by parents eager to have their daughters marry prominent warriors or chiefs for the prestige involved. Frequently the young brides found themselves marrying men who already had one or two wives, which was a perfectly acceptable practice in many tribes since there was a chronic shortage of men. And now and then a maiden would be captured by enemy warriors in a raid, taken back to their village, and made

34

a bride whether she liked the idea or not.

"I hoped you could tell me where she is," Flying Hawk signed forlornly. "That is why I spared you when I should have killed you for shooting two of my friends. I should still kill you, but you impress me as being an upright man. So you may go in peace. But should we ever meet again, know that I will slay you on the spot."

The man's acute desperation was almost contagious. Nate pondered for several seconds, then signed, "Where are your friends? What will you do now?"

"My friends took the bodies of those you killed back to our village. I refuse to go back until I find Smoky Woman." Flying Hawk paused. "While I was searching for sign of False Tongue I came on your tracks and followed them. Now I will continue my hunt."

"All by yourself?"

"My friends will be back in nine or ten sleeps."

"How would you like some help until they return?"

"You?"

"Me."

"Why would you help me, white man? My people and yours have long been enemies."

Nate glanced past the Ute, into the trees, where the warrior's horse was tied. If he was to convince Flying Hawk, he must be completely honest. "I have two reasons. First, False Tongue stole my horse and I want to get it back. On foot I would stand little chance. Riding double with you means we can cover much more ground faster."

"And your other reason?"

"I am a white man, true. But I am also an adopted Shoshone. My wife is Shoshone. I have great respect for the Indian ways." Nate paused to arrange in his head how he would phrase the next sequence of signs. "I do not like to see any man—white or Indian—do evil. What

False Tongue did to your sister was very wrong. He deserves to pay for his wickedness and she must be freed."

In the protracted silence that ensued Nate heard sparrows chirping gaily and the chattering of a squirrel. He couldn't tell by the Ute's impassive features whether his argument had prevailed.

"Your words show you to be a good man," Flying Hawk signed after a bit. "But I do not know if it would be wise for us to join forces."

"Do you happen to know a Ute named Two Owls?"

Flying Hawk blinked. "Yes. He is chief in another village and an important man among my people. Why?"

"He and I joined forces once some moons ago against the Blackfeet. I did not betray his trust. I would not betray yours."

"You are Grizzly Killer?"

"I am."

The warrior came a stride nearer and examined Nate closely. "Two Owls told us about you at a gathering of all our people. He said you are the only white he has ever known whose tongue always speaks the truth. He said you have the body of a white man but the spirit of an Indian."

Nate made no comment. He was recalling how Two Owls had helped him save Shakespeare McNair and another man from a war party of Blackfeet that had penetrated deep into Ute territory.

"Very well," Flying Hawk suddenly declared, thrusting out his arm and resting his hand on Nate's shoulder. Then he signed, "Until we find my sister and your horse we will be as brothers. And perhaps, when this is done, I will go back to my people and tell them the same thing Two Owls did, that not all whites have bad hearts."

Smiling in gratitude, Nate touched the Ute's arm. "You will not regret your decision. Between us we will catch False Tongue and make him pay." He nodded at the fire. "Perhaps you would like some food before we start? I would be happy to share my rabbit."

"Thank you. I accept," Flying Hawk replied. He walked off and picked up his bow and arrow, sliding the latter into the quiver on his back. The bow went over his left shoulder. As he came back he pointed at Nate's wounded shoulder. "I an glad my arrow did not kill you."

In the act of stepping to his weapons, Nate stopped. "*You* were the one who shot me?"

"Yes. I tried to get you through the heart but you ran like an antelope."

"The next time I will try to run slower," Nate joked. He slid the pistol under his belt, recovered the tomahawk and knife, and squatted by the fire, across from the Ute.

"You took the arrow out all by yourself?" the warrior asked, staring at the wound.

"Yes."

Flying Hawk folded his arms on top of his knees. "You have much courage. It is a pity most white men are not like you."

Soon Nate had more chunks of meat roasting over the fire. He picked up the stick he had dropped when the Ute appeared and brushed bits of grass off the pieces of rabbit, then heated them again. Not a word was spoken during the meal. Nate was self-consciously aware that the warrior stared at him the whole time. He, in turn, made it a point to act as natural as he could. Eventually the Ute asked him an unexpected question.

"Will more of your people come to these mountains?"

"Many more, I am afraid. Once the whites who live east of the Great River learn how beautiful and wonderful this land is, they will flock here by the thousands."

David Thompson

Flying Hawk wiped his greasy fingers on his leggins. "I have been told this would happen but I hope you are wrong. My people, as well as the Cheyennes, the Kiowas, the Sioux, and many other tribes will not let your people drive us off. We will fight to keep our land."

"I know."

"On which side will you fight when that happens?"

"I have not given the matter much thought."

"You should."

The man had a point, Nate reflected as he doused the fire. What *would* he do if it came to pass? The mere notion of hordes of settlers spreading out over the plains and the mountains, staking claim to every available square foot of land, was enough to give him the jitters. Part of the appeal the wilderness made to men like him was the virtue of soothing solitude. The vast expanses of shimmering grasslands and towering peaks stirred a man's soul like no towns or cities ever could. Out here a man could live as he pleased, accountable to no one but himself and his Maker. There weren't countless laws to obey, countless rules to follow. Freedom—pure, unadulterated freedom—was there for the taking. All that would change once civilization arrived. A man would be at the mercy of politicians, and to Nate's way of thinking that was a fate worse than death.

With the Hawken tucked under his left arm, he followed the Ute to where the sturdy roan waited. He waited for Flying Hawk to reach down, then swung up behind the warrior.

They rode to the northwest, over hills, through valleys, and around mountains, always on the lookout for tracks. Toward noon they scaled a steep slope, crossed a low saddle, and came out on a splendid high country park lush with spring growth. There Flying Hawk reined up and twisted so Nate could see his hands.

38

"There is a spring here. We will stop and rest my horse, then go on."

At the bottom of a cliff on the north side of the park was a crystal-clear pool of ice-cold water. Nate dropped to the ground, walked to the water's edge, and sank onto all fours to drink. As he lowered his face he happened to glance to his left. His thirst was immediately forgotten. For clearly imbedded in the soft soil were large hoofprints not over a day old. Rising, he signed, "You are closer to your sister than you think. Look at these."

Flying Hawk's face lit up like the full moon. He ran his fingers lightly over the tracks, then stood and slowly walked in a half-circle, reading the sign. "Do you think these were made by your horse?"

"I would say so, yes. I know the tracks of my animal as well as I do my own." Pivoting, Nate gazed the entire length of the park. At the north end reared a seemingly impassable barrier of bleak, barren mountains. Either there was another way out of the park further on, or else Solomon Cain was hiding somewhere near those mountains.

The Ute came to the same conclusion. "We have him, Grizzly Killer. You have brought me luck. After searching for so long I find him this easily."

"Do not get your hopes too high. As you say, False Tongue is exceedingly clever. Who knows where this trail will lead?"

"We shall see."

Flying Hawk pulled the roan away from the spring and climbed up. He impatiently gestured for Nate to join him, and at a gallop they rode northward, the roan's hoofs drumming dully on the thick carpet of grass. Occasionally they saw clear tracks, but for the most part the prints were smudged or partials. Cain, after leaving the spring, had cut catty-corner across the park toward a foreboding mountain crowned by three separate pinnacles of rock that resembled the three prongs of a pitchfork.

They lost the trail at the base of the mountain where the grass gave way to loose rock and hard-packed earth.

The Ute stopped and peered upward. "He must be somewhere up there."

So it seemed, but Nate couldn't see why Cain would have picked such a godforsaken spot to hide out. True, plenty of water and grass was readily available in the park. But the oddly sinister mountain, on which not so much as a single weed or blade of grass grew, was fit neither for man nor beast alike. He looked at Flying Hawk, expecting the warrior to begin climbing at any moment, and was startled when he saw the Ute give a barely perceptible shudder.

"I know this place," Flying Hawk signed. "My people call it the Mountain of Death. No one has ever gone up it and returned."

Nate straightened and smiled. So that was it! The wily Cain had picked a spot taboo to the Utes, using their primitive superstition to his advantage. "Are there eaves on this mountain?" he asked.

"Let us find out."

The lower portion of the facing slope proved easy for the roan. Above it the going was too steep, compelling them to dismount and walk. Small stones clattered out from under their feet. So did small puffs of dust. Their moccasins were caked by the time they came to the mouth of a ravine. In the earth at the entrance were fresh tracks.

"We have him!" Flying Hawk signed excitedly.

Nate hoped so. Once he had Pegasus back he would head for home, tell his wife what had transpired, then resume his search for choice areas to trap beaver far to the northwest. He'd learned his lesson the hard way. Venturing into Ute country was tempting Fate, a notoriously harsh mistress. From now on out, he decided, he would stay shy of Ute territory unless he had a damn good reason for doing otherwise.

In the confined space between the high ravine walls the clopping of the roan was unusually loud. Nate scanned the rims above, bothered at being a potential target should Cain be perched up there with a rifle. He grinned when he spotted the end of the defile and hefted the Hawken.

Flying Hawk had pulled a shaft from his quiver and notched it on the bow string.

A strong breeze struck them, growing in intensity the closer they drew to whatever lay beyond the ravine. Nate tugged his hat down and narrowed his eyes to reduce the bright glare off the ravine walls. Then they were there, and he stopped in midstride on seeing the landscape that unfolded before their astounded eyes.

An arid wasteland of gorges, plateaus, and bluffs formed a virtual maze of inhospitable terrain stretching for miles in all directions. Scattered bushes and scrub trees comprised the only plant life. A solitary golden eagle soared on high on the air currents. Otherwise, nothing moved. The breeze, a hot blast of wind, hit them full force.

"There!" Flying Hawk signed with the bow in his left hand, and pointed using his right.

Nate screened his eyes from the sun, using his palm, and saw the reason the warrior was so excited. Far out in the wasteland rose a thin tendril of white smoke, so faint as to be almost indistinguishable.

"False Tongue!" the Ute said. "Now I know why I could not find him. He is even more clever than I believed." He replaced the arrow, slung the bow, and swiftly mounted. "Hurry, Grizzly Killer. My sister is close. I can feel she is."

Nate mounted also, and the roan broke into a gallop, raising a cloud of dust in their wake. Nate tapped Flying Hawk on the shoulder and bobbed his head at the dust.

Scowling in displeasure, Flying Hawk slowed.

Keeping the smoke in sight proved difficult. Unless the angle of the sun was just right they would lose track of it. Often they had to skirt bluffs, and then had to look hard to find the smoke again when they were in the open. Several times they passed through gorges and were denied sight of the wispy column for minutes on end.

Nate feared the fire would be put out before they got close enough to pinpoint its location. Mile after mile fell behind them. The roan began to tire, its head drooping. Nate himself felt as if he was roasting alive. Often he mopped his brow and ran a hand over his neck. He was sorry now that they hadn't taken the time to drink their full back at the spring in the park.

After two hours of grueling travel Nate was about to advise Flying Hawk to stop and rest when the wind brought to his sensitive nose the acrid aroma of burning wood. The Ute smelled it too, because he stiffened. They rode for another hundred yards, to a point where the dry wash they had been following made a sharp turn to the right around a rise. The smoke appeared to be wafting skyward on the other side.

Flying Hawk drew rein and slid down. He left the roan standing there and beckoned for Nate to make haste.

And Nate did, although he didn't like rushing in when common sense dictated they should go slowly and warily. The element of surprise was essential if they were to take Cain without a fight. That is, if the Ute wanted to avoid bloodshed, which he doubted. He caught up with the warrior as they neared the turn, and they both dropped onto their hands and knees and crawled to where they could see past the rise.

The fire was 50 yards off, outside of the dark mouth to a large cave situated in a rock wall over a hundred feet high. Pegasus and two other horses were tethered outside the cave, in the shade, close to a small pool.

Nate saw a shadowy figure move in the cave mouth, and seconds later a beautiful Indian woman in a beaded buckskin dress, her raven hair flowing down to her hips, emerged carrying a tin pot and walked to the fire.

Flying Hawk could barely contain himself. "That is my sister!" he signed, beaming broadly. "But where is False Tongue?"

Shrugging, Nate scoured the area but saw no trace of the man they sought. Suddenly a shadow fell across them, and glancing up he felt his breath catch in his throat.

Looming tall on the brim of the wash, a cocked flint-lock held steady in each tanned hand, wearing buckskins and moccasins and smirking in triumph, was Solomon Cain.

Chapter
Four

"Payin' a visit, are you?" Solomon Cain asked merrily.

Flying Hawk spun and went to lift his bow, a futile act since all Cain had to do was twitch a forefinger and the Ute would receive a ball in the chest or head. Nate, out of the corner of his eye, saw the warrior spin, and flicked out his hand to stop the bow from rising. Flying Hawk glared at him and tried to tear the bow loose, then froze when Cain spoke sternly in the Ute tongue. Hissing like an enraged viper, the Ute removed his fingers from the bow and held his hands aloft.

"Sensible cuss, ain't he?" Cain addressed Nate in English. "Now why don't you do the same with your guns and such or I'll be obliged to put some lead into your system."

With the twin barrels of those pistols fixed on his person, there was nothing else Nate could do but ease his weapons to the ground.

"Now stand and step out of temptation's reach," Cain ordered, and issued a similar statement in the Ute language.

Side by side, Nate and Flying Hawk backed off.

"I must admit I am surprised," Cain said, giving each of them a firm scrutiny. "I never expected you two dunderheads to ever find me." He jumped from the top of the wash and landed lightly on the balls of his feet, his pistols swiveling to cover them as he dropped.

"You stole my horse, you son of a bitch," Nate growled, more so because he was mad at himself for blundering into Cain's grasp than anything else.

"And a nice horse it is," Cain responded blithely. "Didn't give me a lick of trouble until I came through the ravine. Then it acted up considerably. I guess it wanted to go back to you, but I got it here anyway."

"Too bad Pegasus didn't throw you off and bust your head wide open."

"My, you are in a feisty mood today," Cain quipped, then transferred his attention to Flying Hawk and spoke in Ute. The warrior, flushing crimson, clenched his fists.

"For a fierce Ute he sure has a soft hide," Cain said, and laughed. "All I did was tell him how pretty I think his sister is."

Nate debated whether to try and reach Cain before the man could fire and had to face the truth. He'd be shot down before he took three steps. A distraction was called for. But what? "You may have us," he mentioned when an idea occurred to him, "but the others will get you. There are ten more Utes about a mile behind us. You won't stand a prayer."

"Is that the best you can do?" Cain retorted. "I happened to be up on the rise when I spotted the two of you. And do you know what? I watched and watched and never saw anyone else. How naughty of you to lie like that, King."

45

Thwarted, Nate struggled to remain calm, to not let his anger at being captured gain the upper hand. Only by doing so would he be ready to make his move if an opportunity presented itself. For the time being there was no denying they were completely at Cain's mercy, which meant they might not have long to live. For lack of anything better to do, he elected to try a risky bluff. Putting a grin on his face, he said, "Do you really think the Utes would give themselves away? I thought you knew more about Indians than that."

A hint of uncertainty crept into Cain's eyes.

"Go ahead and shoot," Nate blustered. "They'll hear the shot and come on the run."

"You're lyin' through your teeth."

"Am I? Are you absolutely sure?"

No, Cain wasn't, and his expression conveyed as much. Turning slightly, he shot a glance over his shoulder, then regarded Nate in annoyance. "I ain't goin' to buy your story, King. Not even a little bit." He wagged his pistols. "But I'm not one to play the odds when the stakes are so high. We'll wait and see if more Utes show. If they don't, you and I are goin' to do some chawin' about what happens to them who lie to me."

"Talk about the pot calling the kettle black," Nate taunted.

Solomon Cain motioned with the flintlocks. "I want the two of you to start walkin' to my cave. Walk slow and keep your arms where I can see 'em. If you don't, I can guarantee you'll be sorry." He looked at Flying Hawk and repeated his instructions in the Ute's tongue.

If ever two men were the picture of depression, it had to be Nate and the warrior as they hiked along the wash until it ended, and then climbed out and made for Cain's hideaway. Nate wished he could plant a foot on his own backside for being so careless. He'd acted like a greenhorn and paid the price for his folly. But all was not lost. He'd bought them some time by instilling doubt in Cain about the possible presence of more Utes. Until Cain became convinced the two of them were indeed alone, they were safe unless they gave him cause to shoot.

They had hardly cleared the top of the wash when Smoky Woman spotted them and squealed in delight. Like a doe she bounded toward them and hurled herself into her brother's arms.

Nate halted when Flying Hawk did. He watched the two warmly embrace and heard them exchange a few urgent words. Smoky Woman then glanced at Cain and spoke some more. Cain replied curtly. At that moment Nate would have given anything to be fluent in the Ute tongue. He knew a few words from the time he hooked up with Two Owls, but nowhere near enough to conduct a conversation. For lack of anything else to do, he studied the woman indirectly responsible for their dilemma.

The beauty of youth animated her finely chiseled features. Her eyes were a soft brown, her complexion as smooth as a baby's with nary a wrinkle marring her skin. Her full lips were a tantalizing cherry color, while her full bosom swelled with each breath she took. She was a living work of art, and Nate had no difficulty understanding what Cain saw in her and why Cain had abducted her. If nothing else, the bastard had excellent taste in women. She appeared to be quite upset at her brother being held at gunpoint, but all her arguments were apparently wasted on Cain.

Nate stared at the cave as they neared it. The heady odor of simmering venison filled the air, and he saw that Smoky Woman had stew going. Pegasus, spying Nate, tried to come over, only to be stopped short by the rope. Just inside the cave, piled against the wall, were saddles,

47

parfleches, blankets, and other provisions. "Looks like you plan to be here a spell," he commented.

"Another month or two should do me," Cain responded.

"What then?"

"I go back to St. Louis and buy the biggest mansion there is. The rest of my born days are goin' to be lived in the lap of luxury. Fine food. Fancy clothes. Expensive carriages. You name it, I'll own it."

"It costs a lot of money to do all that," Nate observed.

"I'll have something better than money."

"Such as?"

Cain cackled, or started to, his laugh abruptly changing to a strangled grunt. He stopped for a second, astonishment plain on his face, then he cackled again, only louder. "Why didn't I think of this before?" he declared.

"Think of what?" Nate asked as he came to the fire and turned.

"You'll see soon enough. You and this poor excuse for an Injun," Cain said.

The undisguised contempt in the man's tone troubled Nate, and he looked at Smoky Woman. Arm in arm with her brother, she was speaking so softly the words were nearly inaudible.

"I want both of you to get on your knees and put your hands behind your backs," Cain commanded, then repeated, yet again, the same instruction in the Ute language.

Sighing in reservation, Nate obeyed, but as he swung his hands around he dragged his left hand along the ground and scooped up a small handful of loose dirt. Then he set himself and waited. Once Cain stepped close enough, he was going to hurl the dirt in the polecat's face and tackle him, come what may.

Flying Hawk refused to kneel. Folding his arms, he stood immobile, his chin jutting proudly, and glared at

Cain as if daring Cain to do something.

Cain did. Addressing Smoky Woman in Ute, he took a couple of paces toward her, then abruptly shifted, took a single long bound, and slammed his right flintlock against Flying Hawk's temple. The warrior crumpled. In a burst of sheer savagery, Cain struck the Ute two more times, and would have gone on doing so had not Smoky Woman leaped to her brother's defense and seized hold of Cain's arm.

Nate began to rise, thinking he could pounce before Cain knew what hit him, but the wily Cain spun and extended his free arm, pointing the other pistol straight at Nate's face. Although Nate was boiling like a teapot about to bubble over, he had no choice but to sink back down.

Cain suddenly shook Smoky Woman off and raised his hand as if to cuff her. He was fury incarnate, yet at the last instant he caught himself and slowly lowered his arm to his side. Then he said something to her, something that caused her to bow her head in apparent guilt. Pivoting, she entered the cave, going to the wall where their supplies were piled.

What hold, Nate wondered, did Solomon Cain have over the young woman? Why did she meekly submit when the life of her own brother was in jeopardy? Intuition told him there was more going on here than met the eye.

When Smoky Woman returned she was carrying a coiled rope and a hunting knife. Walking up to Nate, she unwound a length of rope and cut it off. Then she moved behind him.

This was not what Nate had expected. He'd counted on Cain doing the tying. Throwing the dirt in Smoky Woman's face would accomplish nothing, and Cain wasn't quite close enough. Maybe he could remedy that. "Do you always let a woman do all your work for you?" he asked sarcastically.

Cain made a clucking noise. "You must figure I'm a greenhorn, King. I ain't about to get near enough for you to jump me, so forget any hare-brained notions you have. Just go along with what I want and you might live to see that wife and kid you were tellin' me about."

Nate felt his wrists being encircled by loops of rope. "This is so senseless," he remarked. "All I want is my horse, and all Flying Hawk wants is his sister. If you leave her here and ride off, right now, we'll let you go in peace."

"You never stop tryin', do you?" Cain said. "As for your offer, I know better. Flying Hawk ain't the forgivin' kind. Neither, I suspect, are you when it comes to havin' your horse stolen. If I was to ride off, one or both of you would be on my trail before the dust settled. No, thanks." Grinning, he wagged both flintlocks. "We'll keep things the way they are."

Nate shrugged. "I gave you a chance. It's up to you whether you live or die." He gazed at the rise. "I just hope those Utes show up soon."

The reminder had the desired effect. Cain stiffened and half turned to survey the area.

Smoky Woman finished tying Nate's wrists, then bound his ankles. Rising, she took two steps toward her brother. Cain snapped at her and jabbed a flintlock at Nate.

This time it was easy to guess what had been said. Nate saw Smoky Woman flush crimson, then she moved back around him and knelt. He could feel her working at the rope, loosening the knots, but only so she could bind him much tighter than before, so tight the rope bit into his skin. Cain, Nate deduced, had been afraid she wouldn't do a proper job. Perhaps Cain reasoned she might deliberately leave enough slack for them to eventually slip free. Now they wouldn't be able to. The man, evidently, always thought of everything.

Dejected, Nate watched the woman tie her brother. Flying Hawk groaned when she gently touched him. A tear formed in the corner of her eye, yet she made no move to brush it away until the deed was done. Rising, she took the knife and the remainder of the rope into the cave.

"I'm goin' to leave you in her capable hands while I go have a look-see for these Utes you keep talkin' about," Cain said. "But don't do anything stupid 'cause I'm pickin' up your weapons on the way. That includes your fine Hawken. If you move from that spot, I'll shoot you with your own gun. And believe me when I say I'm a tolerable shot with a rifle."

Nate believed him. Frontiersmen, by virtue of necessity, had to become adept. Those who couldn't shoot straight seldom survived run-ins with hostiles and were hard-pressed to fill their bellies. So Cain's threat was no idle boast, especially since a Hawken was one of the most accurate guns ever made. Some trappers liked to joke that a Hawken was so good it aimed itself.

Cain wedged his pistols under his belt and commented, "Don't look so glum, King. You're still alive, which ought to count for something."

Watching the man hasten off, Nate speculated on Cain's purpose in holding them as prisoners. There was no rhyme or reason to it that he could see. Cain would have to keep his eyes on them the whole time, knowing full well if one of them broke loose he was a dead man. Not that Nate was complaining. So long as he lived he would continually try to escape.

Shortly Flying Hawk revived with a start and sat up. He looked around, spotted Cain, then rotated on his backside and spoke harshly to his sister, going on at some length. Smoky Woman listened with her chin lowered. Twice she gave one-word replies. When, after a while, Flying Hawk gestured with his bound arms for her to cut him loose, she mumbled a few words, rose and hurried inside, leaving her brother to gape in disbelief.

Nate sadly shook his head. How strange Fate could be! he reflected. What cruel jokes it played! Here he was, held prisoner by a white man he had befriended, in the company of an Indian who hated all whites and had put an arrow into him, while the Indian's sister, who they had come to rescue and who could free them then and there if she wanted, refused to help. He would have laughed if he wasn't feeling so miserable.

The Ute, sliding his legs under him, began to rise.

Nate looked and realized Cain had disappeared into the wash. Flying Hawk probably thought it was safe for him to stand. But Cain might reappear at any instant, and if the warrior was on his feet Cain would undoubtedly shoot him. Nate shook his head and started to warn Flying Hawk about Cain's threat. The next second, though, Smoky Woman practically flew from the cave and pushed her brother down again.

Irate, Flying Hawk barked at her and she responded in kind. Again the warrior attempted to rise. Again she shoved him back.

So engrossed did Nate become in their bickering that he failed to see Cain emerge from the wash. When next he glanced in that direction he was surprised to find Cain a third of the way up the rise. "Hey!" Nate said to get the attention of the Utes. When he had it, he bobbed his head at Cain, certain once Flying Hawk saw Cain with a rifle he would know not to stand up.

The warrior appeared on the verge of throwing a fit. Instead, he verbally lashed his sister, bringing moisture to both of her eyes. Wheeling, she walked off, over to the horses, and stood with her back to her brother.

Nate knew Flying Hawk blamed Smoky Woman for foiling his escape, when in reality she had saved his life.

The last thing they needed was to antagonize her. But he was helpless to change the situation since he had no way of communicating with his hands tied.

So he sat and brooded. He saw Cain reach the top of the rise and hunker down at a vantage point that afforded a bird's-eye view of the cave and them. The man then had the brazen gall to smile and give a cheery wave.

It was hot there, under the blistering sun, and Nate sweated freely. He looked longingly at the pool and licked his lips. As the minutes dragged by it occurred to him that Cain might stay up there for a long time to be absolutely certain there were no other Utes around. He glanced at Smoky Woman and said, "Pardon me, but could you fetch me a some water to drink?"

She stood like a statue, unhearing, too upset over her clash with her brother to care about anything else.

Nate had to think a bit before he recollected the Ute word for hello. He now tried that, but she still didn't budge. Again he said it, louder this time, almost shouting.

At last Smoky Woman glanced around to regard him quizzically.

Smiling his friendliest smile, Nate indicated the pool and made a show of swallowing in great gulps. She understood right away. Going into the cave, she returned bearing a large tin cup which she filled and brought over. But not to Nate. First she stopped beside her brother and held the cup close to his mouth.

Flying Hawk deliberately turned his face away.

Her slender shoulders sagging, Smoky Woman stepped to Nate's side and touched the cool tin to his lips.

Nate drank gratefully, draining the entire cup. Some of the water spilled over the brim, across his chin, and down his neck, providing additional relief. When he was done, he beamed and absently said in English, "Thank you."

"You welcome," Smoky Woman replied softly.

David Thompson

Surprise made Nate gape. Then he realized she had been with Cain for four months. It was inevitable she would have picked up some of the language in that time. "You are very kind," he said quickly as she turned to go. "This all must be very hard on you."

"Yes," she said, staring morosely into the empty cup.

Nate didn't want her to leave. If he could get her talking, if he could befriend her, she might become an ally in his campaign to free himself. And too, he might be able to learn what Cain was up to, which she must know. So when she took a step, he blurted out, "Wait! Please!"

Smoky Woman paused, then faced him.

"I am sorry your brother is so mad at you. He doesn't know that you were saving his life. But I do. And I admire you for it. If I spoke enough of your tongue I'd tell him, but I know very little."

"I know little English," Smoky Woman said, pronouncing the last word "Ainlish."

"You do right fine," Nate complemented her. "My tongue isn't easy to learn." His racing mind hit on a way to solicit her sympathy. "My wife speaks it fluently, but then she's got more brains in her little finger than I do in my whole body."

"You have wife?" Smoky Woman asked as if deeply disturbed by the news.

"A wife and a fine young son," Nate disclosed. "I love them both with all my heart, and I surely do hope I get to see them again."

Her sadness intensified. "What your name?"

"Nate King. Or you can call me Grizzly Killer."

"Why you here?"

"I came to help your brother save you. Flying Hawk must love you as much as I do my wife because he has never stopped hunting for you. He's never given up hope. The whole time you've been with Cain, your brother and his friends have been scouring the countryside."

She pursed her lips and surreptitiously looked at the warrior. "We close. He good man."

Here was an opening Nate thought he could exploit. "And Solomon Cain? Is he a good man?"

Smoky Woman's face darkened ominously. "Not talk about him."

"I'm sorry. Don't be upset. I didn't know you cared for him. Flying Hawk led me to believe Cain took you against your will, and I just naturally figured you wouldn't like him much."

"Not talk about Cain!"

Nate was shocked at how upset she was. He'd inadvertently angered her, and the fragile bridge of friendship he was trying to build threatened to collapse around his ears. "Again, I'm truly sorry," he said quickly, frantically seeking another subject to talk about. The mouthwatering aroma from the stew gave him inspiration. "Please forgive me," he said, and grinned. "I need to stay in your good graces so you'll give me some of that stew of yours. It smells delicious."

She stared into the cup again.

"Your cooking reminds me of my wife's," Nate went on. "She can turn a pot of water and meat into the tastiest concoction this side of Heaven. Some women have the knack, I guess. Me, I'm happy if I cook a meal where half the food isn't burned."

His humor was wasted on her. Frowning, she lowered the cup and glanced at the cave.

"How far back does that go?" Nate inquired before she could leave.

"Far."

"It must be a bit dank and dreary in there," Nate mentioned. "Caves are fit for bats and vermin, not people. I bet it's nothing at all like living in a lodge, is it?"

55

"It all right. Keep us dry when rain, warm when night."

"Well, bears seem to put great store by caves, so I suppose living in one does have its advantages," Nate commented.

"People live here. Many winters ago."

"What's that?" Nate responded, unsure whether he comprehended. "Do you mean other people have lived in this same cave?"

"Yes. They paint walls. Paint buffalo. Paint other things."

"I'd like to see for myself," Nate said, genuinely interested. He'd heard rumors of trappers occasionally finding evidence of an unknown people who had lived in the land long, long ago, but he had yet to see any evidence for himself. Adding to the mystery, some Indian tribes claimed their ancestors had encountered strange people back in the dawn of antiquity, back in the earliest days of remembered Indian history, which was passed down from generation to generation by word of mouth. These mysterious ancient ones had resented the inroads of the Indians and been exterminated in ruthless warfare. Or so the tales went. He was going to ask about the cave paintings when he heard the crunch of footsteps and he looked over his shoulder to see a grim Solomon Cain approaching.

Chapter
Five

Nate had no idea why Cain wore the look of a man who wanted to kill someone, but it was not at all hard to guess *who* Cain wanted to slay. The man's flinty eyes bored into him like twin knives, and he had the impression Cain was going to attack him as soon as he came close enough. Since in his helpless state he would be unable to ward off an attack, he managed a smile and said innocently, "Back so soon?"

"What have the two of you been jawin' about?" Cain demanded, with a sharp glance at Smoky Woman.

"Nothing much," Nate said.

Cain halted in front of him and fingered the Hawken, as if contemplating whether to pound the stock down on Nate's head. "I want a straight answer," he snapped.

"We talked about her brother being mad at her," Nate said, keeping up his air of innocence. "And she told me about the paintings in the cave."

"That was all?" Cain inquired suspiciously.

"Pretty much. Why?"

"I don't want you talkin' to her when I'm not around."

"How was I to know? You never told me."

Cain's brow knit for a moment. Then, apparently appeased, he slowly lowered the Hawken to his side. "No, I didn't. But I'm tellin' you now. Don't do it again." He rested the butt end of the rifle on the ground and idly wrapped his fingers around the barrel. "If I was you, King, I'd do everything I could to get free. Which is why I wouldn't put it past you to try and fill her head with unflatterin' notions about me."

Nate, gazing past Cain, saw Flying Hawk tense his entire body, the warrior's muscles standing out like iron cords. What was the Ute up to? he wondered.

"You're stuck here until I decide otherwise," Cain was saying. "So you might as well—"

In an explosive burst of speed, Flying Hawk threw himself onto the ground and rolled, his body a blur as he barreled into Cain's legs and upended their captor.

Nate, seated in front of Cain, was unable to move aside in time to avoid being flattened when Cain toppled on top of him. As they fell, the Hawken's barrel struck him a jarring blow on the jaw, causing pinpoints of light to flare before his eyes. He felt Cain's weight on top of him and heard the man's furious curses. Twisting and squirming, he tried to disentangle himself. A fist to the chin stopped him.

Stunned, he barely heard the sounds of a strenuous commotion. Dimly he realized Cain and Flying Hawk were struggling beside him. A flying elbow accidentally jarred his side. A lashing foot caught him on the shin. Then his vision returned to normal and he rolled onto his side, planning to aid the Ute. He was too late.

Solomon Cain, his features flushed crimson with rage, was astride Flying Hawk's chest and flailing away like a madman, raining punch after punch on the warrior's unprotected face. Flying Hawk's lips were split and blood poured from his nose, but Cain still wasn't letting up. He whipped his arm on high for another savage swing.

Suddenly Smoky Woman was there, seizing Cain's arm and holding fast to prevent him from striking her brother again. She cried out, "No! Please! No more!"

For a second Nate thought the enraged Cain was going to hit her, but a peculiar expression, almost one of shock, came over Cain and his fists gradually unclenched. His body lost its tension as he gulped in air. She reached out to stroke his cheek, whispering, "Thank you."

"Damn him," Cain said hoarsely. "He made me do it. If he'd behave himself, this wouldn't happen."

"I know."

Nate was appalled by Smoky Woman's attitude. She should be incensed at the pounding Flying Hawk had suffered, but she was more concerned about Cain's feelings. What kind of person was she that she could so callously disregard her own flesh and blood?

Cain turned and stared accusingly at him. "You were party to this, weren't you? It was your job to distract me while he knocked me down."

"I had no idea he was going to do what he did," Nate said.

"Liar! Do you take me for a simpleton? You were fixin' to knock me out, take my knife, and cut yourselves free."

"I'm telling you the truth."

"And horses can fly!" Cain declared. "If I didn't need you, King, I'd shoot you right here and now. As it is, you stay healthy so long as you don't pull a dumb stunt like this again. If you do, you'll be sorry."

Recognizing the futility of disputing the accusation, Nate sat quietly and waited for Cain's wrath to spend itself.

"This is what I get for going easy on you. I should have beaten you some to show you what would happen if you acted up. If only I had a pair of shackles or leg irons, I'd fix your hash! But I guess I'll have to make do."

Smoky Woman interrupted, pointing at her bloody brother. "May I help him?"

"No!" Cain barked, snapping upright. He picked up the Hawken, then grabbed her by the wrist and stormed off into the cave, vanishing around a bend.

Nate promptly sidled over to Flying Hawk. The warrior was conscious but badly battered; his lips had been smashed, his nose was bleeding profusely, and his left eyebrow had been split open. "Are you all right?" Nate asked, knowing Flying Hawk couldn't understand the words but hoping his tone would suffice to convey his worry.

The Ute pushed off the ground and shook his head a few times as if to clear it, his mane of black hair flying. Then he looked at Nate and the corners of his bleeding mouth tugged slightly upward.

Smiling at the warrior's indomitable spirit, Nate sat up. He was sweating profusely again and his mouth was dry. Lying in the dust nearby was the tin cup, but it might as well be lying on the moon. He glanced at the inviting spring, and longed to be able to go over and enjoy a refreshing drink. Rather than torment himself with the impossible, he turned away and gazed forlornly at the slate-blue sky.

Flying Hawk's stunt was bound to make escape harder, he reflected. Cain would be more cautious from then on out, seldom if ever giving them the chance they needed. It was wiser to play along for the time being, to put Cain off guard. Yet how could he convince the Ute of that when he couldn't even employ sign language until his hands were loose? There was no way.

Dejected, Nate listened to the gusty wind coming from the northwest and waited for Cain to reappear. He had a long wait. The broiling sun climbed steadily higher and higher. By his estimation an hour went by, then two. His thirst progressively worsened. Now and again he debated whether to sit back to back with Flying Hawk so he could try to untie the warrior, but he never carried through with the thought. The risk was too great. At any moment Cain might emerge.

The afternoon was half over when their captor finally strolled into the sunlight. He wore two pistols and his knife and had his thumbs hooked under his belt. "Gets hot here, don't it?" he remarked, strolling over. "Hot as an oven."

"I don't mind," Nate lied, straightening and composing himself. He refused to give Cain the satisfaction of seeing him in misery.

"Sort of reminds me of the desert," Cain said. "The heat there can roast a man alive in a day or so if he ain't careful. You ever been to the desert, King?"

"Not yet."

"I have. It's no place for greenhorns. There are scorpions that can kill a man with stingers no longer than your little fingernail. There are rattlers that move all funny-like, from side to side instead of goin' along in a straight line. There are toads as big as rabbits. And there are ugly lizards that bite down on a man so hard he can't ever get 'em off. All sorts of strange critters live there."

"How interesting."

Cain sighed. "Here I am tryin' to be civil and you act like you hate the sight of me."

"I do."

"Would you feel different if I said that I'm sorry I blew up earlier? Hell, you've got to admit I had good reason. Now I want us to be on speakin' terms again.

61

Is there anything wrong with that?"

Nate motioned with his arms. "Not at all. And since you're in such a kind mood, cut me free and I promise to behave myself."

"I can't do that."

"Figured as much."

"You just don't understand."

"Enlighten me then," Nate prompted, utterly perplexed by Cain's erratic behavior. Two hours ago the man had been primed to blow his brains out. Now Cain was acting as if they should be the best of friends. Perhaps his previous hunch was correct; Cain wasn't right in the head.

"I suppose it is time at that," Cain remarked. Drawing his knife, he leaned over to slash the rope binding Nate's ankles. He did the same with Flying Hawk. Then, before either of them could stand, he glided to one side and drew a pistol. The knife went back in its sheath and the other pistol took its place.

Nate heard the distinctive metallic clicks as both hammers were cocked simultaneously, and he looked up into the menacing barrel pointed at his forehead. "I hope you don't sneeze," he said.

A cold smile was Cain's reply. "On your feet, both of you," he directed. "Slowly, please."

As Nate complied the same order was given to Flying Hawk, who jumped up and stood with his eyes fixed in hatred on Cain. Nate feared the warrior would commit another rash act, but Flying Hawk made no aggressive moves.

"Here's what we're goin' to do," Cain said. "I want you to walk ahead of me into the cave. When I tell you to stop, stop. Don't try any tricks or you won't see daylight again." As usual, he translated his statement for the Ute's benefit.

Nate turned and took the lead. He saw Smoky Woman standing contritely near the entrance. For some reason she refused to meet his gaze when he went by her.

The interior of the cave was spacious, 15 feet from wall to wall and ten feet from the ground to the ceiling. Someone had dug out regularly spaced niches in the walls for candles, only a few of which were currently lit. Past the supplies the passageway turned to the right.

Nate rounded the corner and stopped short in surprise. The passage widened, forming a large chamber lit by a bright lantern. To the right lay thick buffalo robes for sleeping purposes. To the left, propped against the wall, were picks, shovels, chisels, and other tools. Directly ahead, where the chamber narrowed again, was a huge pile of pale rocks and dirt. Near the pile were a half-dozen closed packs.

"Figure it out yet?" Cain asked.

"No," Nate admitted.

"You will soon," Cain said, and snickered. He spoke in Ute.

Smoky Woman walked across the chamber, knelt by a pack, and opened the flap. Taking out a rock, she returned and held it out in the palm of her hand for Nate to see.

In the glow of the lantern the brilliant yellow hue was unmistakable. With a start Nate realized he was gazing on a treasure few men had ever beheld, a solid gold nugget the size of a hen's egg. He glanced at the bulging packs, the full implications hitting him with the force of a physical blow. Behind him Cain laughed.

"I reckon you understand now."

"*All* those packs?" Nate blurted.

"Yep." Cain stepped in front of them and gazed at the nugget, caressing it with his eyes. "It's taken me months to dig out that much. About broke my back doin' it too." He waved a pistol at the tunnel beyond the pile. "And there's more where that came from, tons of gold in a vein of quartz, the richest find ever."

"How did you find it?"

"Over a year ago I was out lookin' for beaver with my partner, Simon. We found that park and were scoutin' around for a way out the other side when we came on the ravine. I wanted to go back but Simon voted to go on. Am I glad he did." Cain chuckled. "Well, we started across this hellhole toward the mountains to the west. The way we saw it, no one had ever been in this part of the country and the beaver in those mountains would be ripe for the takin'. Then, about the time we laid eyes on this cave, a thunderstorm came along and drove us to cover."

Nate was trying to calculate the wealth those packs must contain, the total soaring into the millions. If Cain was to head for St. Louis at that very minute, he'd still be one of the wealthiest men on the continent, perhaps wealthier than John Jacob Astor, the king of the fur trade, widely acknowledged as the richest man in America.

"We found some old brush in here and got a fire goin'. Simon took to pokin' around, carryin' a firebrand with him so he could see. The next I knew, he was screamin' like the Devil himself was after his soul and I ran on back to see why." Cain paused, his face aglow with the memory. "My eyes about bugged out when I saw all the gold. We knew we were rich. Anything we wanted would be ours. You have no notion of how that felt. Why, we whooped and hollered so loud we about lost our voices."

"What then?" Nate asked. Despite his dislike for Cain he was fascinated by the tale.

"We chipped off a few nuggets and went on out for the supplies we'd need," Cain answered. "Got back here about five months ago and set right to work."

"Where's your partner now?"

The joy on Cain's face drained away, leaving his skin ashen, his lips compressed. "I don't rightly know."

Nate's first reaction was to suspect Cain of lying. Since the dawn of time men had fought and died to possess the precious metal. Wealthy Egyptians, it was said, had been the first to go gold crazy. They had adorned themselves in gold collars, gold bracelets, gold necklaces, gold rings, and other gold jewelry as a symbol of their status. In the Middle Ages alchemists had tried to make gold from lead and mercury. The Spanish had scoured the world for the mythical El Dorado, a land where gold was supposedly as common as sand. Gold was the treasure of treasures. Because of the value placed on it, men would do anything to obtain some. Greed and gold went hand in hand. Lying, stealing, even killing were justified in the eyes of those who craved the metal. How natural, then, that Cain had let greed overwhelm him. He abruptly realized the man was speaking.

"You don't believe me."

"I didn't say that."

"You don't have to say a word. Your face gives you away." Cain made a low hissing noise and began pacing back and forth. "What you think shouldn't matter to me one way or the other, but it does. I didn't kill Simon, King, if that's what you're thinkin'. He up and vanished without a trace."

"Leaving all this gold behind?"

Cain whirled on Nate and leveled both flintlocks. "Damn your bones! Simon was like a brother to me. We'd trapped together for pretty near six years. He saved my hide plenty of times and I did the same for him." He gestured angrily at the packs. "Take a good look. There's enough gold there for ten men. Why would I mind sharin' with him? Tarnation, man! I needed him to help get the gold out."

The sincerity in Cain's voice was real. And Cain was right about needing a partner, Nate conceded. It wouldn't be smart for a lone man to try and pack that much gold safely out of the mountains and all the way to St. Louis or wherever. The going would be slow, taking weeks longer than usual. Traversing some of the steep, narrow trails would be downright hazardous. And once on the prairie, out in the open where roving war parties could easily spot him, a lone rider would be easy pickings.

Cain's indignation had subsided and he had lowered the pistols. "A little over four months ago it happened," he said softly. "We were doin' real fine 'til then, minin' more ore than we figured we would. At the rate we were goin', we aimed to mine for another two months and then head for civilization." He gave a shudder as if cold. "There hadn't been any trouble at all. The Utes, near as we could tell, never came anywhere near this place. We had it all to ourselves. Or so we thought until Simon found the footprints."

"What footprints?"

"Down by the wash. Clear as day, right there in the dirt, was a line of tracks. Whoever made 'em had been barefoot. He'd come out of the wash and stood there starin' at the cave for a spell, then went back into the wash and ran off. We backtracked him a mile or so, but lost the tracks on rocky ground."

"It must have been a Ute," Nate speculated.

"You ever see an Ute go around barefoot?" Cain responded. "The young'uns do, but the adults all wear moccasins." He paused. "Anyway, the feet weren't right for an Ute."

"How so?"

"Indian feet ain't much different than ours. These tracks were made by somebody with short, wide feet, shorter and wider than I ever seen."

"Did the tracks show up again?"

Cain swallowed hard. "The day Simon vanished. We'd worked late the night before and I was tuckered out, so I slept in later than usual. Simon got up first, afore daylight,

66

and went out to make coffee. I remember catchin' a whiff of it and thinkin' of how good it would taste."

Nate listened closely.

"I dozed off again, and when next I woke up I knew something was wrong. Don't ask me how. I just knew. So I jumped out of bed and went outside to find Simon. The first thing I saw was the sun, two hours high if it was a minute. Simon would never have let me sleep in that long." Cain licked his lips. "Then I saw the pack animals were gone, all three of 'em, and our saddle horses were loose. I started yellin' for Simon but he never answered."

If a piece of rock had fallen from the ceiling Nate would have jumped a foot.

"I couldn't figure it out. Right away I went after the horses and brought 'em back. As I was leadin' 'em to the spring I came on the tracks, more of the barefoot kind, only this time there had been six or seven of 'em, and they'd come off the rise instead of out of the wash."

"And your partner?"

Cain spoke so low he could barely be heard. "I found his tracks by the fire where he'd squatted while he got the coffee goin'. He'd had his back to the rise, and I expect he never saw the ones who grabbed him. 'Cause that's what they did. Snuck up on him and took him off, and him a big, strappin' son of a gun who could lick his weight in wildcats."

Nate no longer believed Cain had killed Simon. He was sure Cain was telling the truth for once. The hint of fear in the man's eyes was proof of that.

"I got my rifle and ran on up to the top of the rise, but there was no sign of anyone. Whoever they were, they'd taken our pack animals and Simon and done it all so quiet I never heard a thing." Cain slowly shook his head in evident disbelief. "I don't know why they didn't take our horses too, unless maybe the horses broke loose and they couldn't bother to round 'em up 'cause they wanted to get out of here quick-like."

"Did you backtrack them?"

"I tried. But it was the same old story. The trail led to rocky ground and I lost the sign again."

"And you stayed on after that? Didn't you think they might come back for you?"

"I'm no fool, King. It was all I thought about for the next few days. I didn't hardly know what to do. Leavin' didn't seem right. I kept hopin' Simon would show, and the notion of cuttin' out made me feel guilty, like I was yellow or something. But after a while I got to thinkin' and knew he was never goin' to come back. Whoever took him had killed him. And since I wasn't partial to sharin' his fate, I decided to pack up all the gold we'd mined so far and head out of these infernal mountains."

"What stopped you?"

"Two things. First off, I only had the two saddle horses and they ain't used to carryin' heavy packs. Second, if I loaded both of 'em with the gold I'd have to walk and it's a far piece to Missouri." Cain was calm again, his voice rising. "I knew there was Utes in this region, so I figured on stealin' some of their horses to use as pack animals. The first village I came on was Smoky Woman's. I saw her and some other women off a ways from the lodges, and I started to swing on around 'em when I got a good look at her." He smiled. "I tell you, I never saw any woman so pretty in all my life. I knew I had to have her, and hang the horses till another time."

Nate glanced at the lovely Ute, who was staring at her brother. "So you brought her here? As dangerous as it is?"

"Where else could I take her?" Cain countered. "Besides, with her here the cave felt more like a home than a hole in the ground. And you know what? I wasn't

so worried about those barefoot fellas anymore. Havin'
her for company made me remember I'm a man." He
puffed up his chest. "I'd only leave her for short spells
to go out and hunt down a deer or whatever. This last
time Flying Hawk and his band found me. And now you
know the whole story."

"Have your visitors returned?"

"Not that I know of. Every mornin' I take a look all
around but I've not seen a single track. The way I figure
it, they were happy with Simon and the pack animals and
they won't be back this way again for a long while."

"What if you're wrong?"

Cain grinned wickedly and tapped Nate's chest with
a pistol. "That's why you're here."

Chapter Six

Nate didn't like the sound of that one bit. "What do you mean?" he asked.

"I refuse to be run off by a pack of murderin' savages who don't even have enough sense to wear something on their feet when they're walkin' on hot rock. I don't know what tribe they belong to, but it doesn't matter. I aim to mine a few more packs of gold before I leave here, and you're goin' to help me."

"Don't count on it."

"Oh?" Cain said, and stepping up to Flying Hawk he touched the end of the flintlock barrel to the Ute's forehead. "You'll either help me or I'll put a hole in your Injun friend."

The warrior, Nate noticed, had not batted an eye. Nate glanced at Smoky Woman, thinking she would protest, but she stood docilely, her features downcast.

"I've got it all worked out," Cain bragged, lowering the pistol. "If the ones who took Simon come back, we can hold 'em off easy. And with the two of us workin', we can dig out all the ore I need in half the time it would take me by my lonesome. So I get out of here that much sooner."

"And when the time comes, what about us?"

"I'm takin' Smoky Woman with me. Flying Hawk and you can go wherever you want."

"Just like that?" Nate said skeptically.

"Sort of. I'm not dumb enough to give your weapons back when I know full well what you'd do to me. No, I'll likely tie you up before I ride out, but not so tight you can't get free after a while, which will give me the head start I need. And I'll leave your Hawken and such in the ravine that leads into the park for you to find once you get there. How's that sound?"

You expect me to believe you? Nate wanted to say, but he didn't. Cain had already shown his true colors once, and Nate wasn't about to trust the man a second time. "Seems to me it doesn't matter what I think. You've given me no choice but to do as you want."

"Keep that in mind and we'll get along dandy," Cain said. He took several steps backward, then glanced at Smoky Woman. "Untie him. He has some work to do."

Covered by the two flintlocks, Nate stood still while the young woman removed the rope. Bringing his hands in front of him, he rubbed his sore wrists and awaited Cain's pleasure.

"I want you to go fetch the horse you rode in on and put it with the others. And don't dawdle. There's a lot to do."

"You'll let me walk on out of here all by myself?" Nate remarked.

"Why shouldn't I? I know your type, King. You're an honorable man. You're not about to ride off when you know I'll shoot Flying Hawk if you don't come back. So off with you. And be quick about it."

Nate was a prisoner of his own principles. Cain had
him pegged perfectly. He wouldn't do anything to endanger the Ute, even though the two of them could hardly be
called friends, and so long as Cain had the upper hand
there was nothing he could do. Turning, he walked out
of the cave, squinting in the brilliant sunshine, and across
to the wash. A glance back showed Smoky Woman at the
cave entrance, watching him, perhaps at Cain's request.

Going to the bottom of the wash, he hurried along
until he came to where Cain had surprised them. A pair
of objects lying to one side caused him to halt in surprise,
then he darted forward and scooped up Flying Hawk's
bow and full quiver. For a man who seldom made mistakes, Solomon Cain had made a big one. Perhaps, Nate
reasoned, Cain hadn't wanted to be burdened with the
bow and quiver after taking the Hawken and cramming
all their other weapons under his belt. Now he could turn
the tables on the bastard.

Or could he? Nate hefted the bow and pondered. It
wasn't as if he could conceal the bow on his person
and get close enough to Cain to use it. And since he
didn't have much experience as an archer, he might
miss anyway. Viewed realistically, the bow did him
little good. Either he hid it somewhere to use later if
the opportunity presented itself, or he took it back with
him. He didn't want to just leave it lying in the wash, at
the mercy of the elements. Warriors had to work many
hours to produce quality bows, and this was as fine a
one as he'd ever seen.

Slinging the bow over his right shoulder and the quiver over his left, he resumed hiking. The horse was where
it should be, sweaty and impatient to get out of the sun.
Leading it by the rope rein, he headed back. Riding
would have been faster, but he wanted time to think.
There had to be a way to trick Cain, to disarm the man or
kill him if necessary. He could throw dirt in Cain's eyes,

or maybe jump on Cain when the man wasn't looking, or simply rush him and hope Cain missed. All involved an aspect of risk that couldn't be avoided. Whichever way he picked, he must be sure when he struck, absolutely sure he stood an even chance of prevailing.

As he walked, he gazed out over the wasteland at the jumble of boulders, gorges, and ridges to the west. The distance to the next range of mountains, he judged, was no more than five miles, twice as far as the distance between the mountains to the east and the cave. He wondered if any white men had ever visited that mysterious range, and imagined the streams and rivers overflowing with beaver. Perhaps, he reflected, after this was all over he would pay those peaks a visit.

He came to the turn and made for the cave. Suddenly he stopped, his eyes narrowing, puzzled by a man-like shape silhouetted on a ridge half a mile away. He couldn't determine if it was the trunk of a tree or a slender column of rock. Then the shape moved and he knew it was neither.

Nate instinctively lowered his hands to his belt, his fingers closing on thin air. He watched breathlessly as the figure moved to the right. It was a man, a man watching him! A tingle of apprehension rippled through him as he realized it must be one of the savages who had taken Cain's partner.

The figure abruptly disappeared.

Nate blinked and questioned whether he had really seen what he thought he saw. It was easy for the eyes to play tricks on a man in the wilderness; heat, elevation, shadows, distance, they all conspired to fool even the most sharp-eyed trappers and warriors. This time, however, he felt he had not been deceived.

Had the strange Indians returned for Cain and the remaining horses? Or was there just the one? Should they anticipate an attack? These and other worries occupied him until he reached the spring and permitted Flying Hawk's horse to drink. Then he stepped over to Pegasus, and was rewarded with a muzzle in the face.

"I've missed you too," Nate whispered, stroking the Palouse's neck and scratching lightly behind its ears.

"My, my. Ain't this a touchin' sight!"

Nate didn't bother to turn. He kept on rubbing Pegasus and commented, "Your visitors are back."

"What?"

"I saw someone on a ridge to the west of us. He was too far off to make out clearly, but I figure it was one of the same band that took your partner."

"You're lyin'. You didn't see anyone."

Turning, Nate met Cain's defiant stare calmly. "Not everybody is like you. Some of us make it a habit to always tell the truth."

The insult was effective. Bristling, Cain advanced a few strides, then caught himself. He'd tucked the pistols under his belt again, but now he drew one and gestured angrily. "Why'd you bring back the bow?"

Nate, wondering why Cain had changed the subject, started toward the entrance. "Flying Hawk might want to use it later to kill you," he replied.

"Drop it, and the quiver."

"What about the man I saw?" Nate asked, pausing long enough to deposit both items at his feet.

"I'm not convinced you did see someone. And even if you did, it could have been an Ute or an Arapaho or a Cheyenne or even a Navajo."

"The Navajo never come this far north," Nate said. "And the Arapahos and Cheyennes never come this far west."

"They might every so often," Cain stated with a total lack of conviction. Gazing westward, he gnawed on his lower lip. "It doesn't matter one way or the other who or what you saw. We're not leavin' until we have enough gold to suit me, and that's final. I know there's a risk involved, but I'd put my own ma at risk if it meant the difference between livin' out my days like old King Midas or windin' up poor and miserable."

At that juncture Smoky Woman emerged and went to Cain's side. She studiously avoided looking at Nate.

"What are we going to do at night? Take turns standing guard?" Nate inquired. "We'll be inviting trouble if we don't. I suggest we each keep watch for three or four hours at a stretch. That way all of us will get some sleep."

"You'd like that!" Cain declared. "If I fell asleep while you were on watch, I'd wake up with my head split open if I woke up at all. No, we won't bother to keep watch. Whoever these Injuns are, they haven't gone into the cave yet. I figure they're scared to enter. We're safe inside."

"You hope. But what if you're wrong?"

Cain shrugged. "You'd better pray I'm not." Motioning for Nate to precede him into the passage, he said, "Right now I've got something I want to show you. Walk slow and keep your hands where I can see 'em at all times."

In the main chamber Nate found Flying Hawk trussed up on the floor, his ankles bound as before. "Was this necessary?"

"It was if I don't want to be lookin' over my shoulders every minute of every day," Cain answered. "He'll kill me first chance he gets and I ain't about to give him that chance." Cain smirked. "Don't worry, though. He'll be untied to eat twice a day. I wouldn't want to upset you by starvin' him to death."

"You're quite the Good Samaritan."

"Just keep walkin'."

Nate went past the huge pile of quartz and dirt and into a narrow tunnel only seven feet high. A lantern

75

suspended from a rock chisel that had been pounded into one wall afforded ample illumination. In moments he came on the vein, situated on the left-hand side at chest height, and saw where Cain and Simon had removed the ore. The wide vein of sparkling white quartz, streaked as it was with liberal clusters and pockets of gleaming gold, dazzled him. There was so much gold in the vein that it imbued the quartz with a yellowish tint. He couldn't help himself. He gaped in awe.

"That's about how I looked the first time I laid eyes on it," Cain mentioned. "I thought I must be dreamin'."

Like all free trappers who had spent many an hour yarning around crackling campfires with boon companions, Nate had heard the many fantastic stories about the tremendous wealth just waiting to be found in the far-flung Rockies. It was common knowledge that the Spanish had operated many fabulous gold and silver mines in the mountains, and most of those mines had still been producing when the Spanish had been forced to retreat southward by hostile tribes and other factors. Thinking they would be back to continue their mining operations, the Spanish had cleverly concealed their mines, but left tantalizing clues carved into rocks and trees to help them relocate the sites when they returned. But they never did return.

In recent years quite a few trappers had discovered such markings, but as yet no one had found one of the lost mines. Because legend had it that there had been so many, several dozen at least, the trappers logically concluded there must be other gold and silver deposits still waiting to be found by anyone lucky enough to stumble across them.

And here was one, right in front of Nate. He reached out, tentatively, and touched a streak of smooth gold.

"Beautiful, ain't it?" Cain said.

"Yes."

"And it's all mine."

The spell was broken. Nate glanced sharply at his captor and said, "You're a fool, Solomon."

"Oh?"

"Yes. There's enough gold here to make ten people rich. You didn't have to force anyone to work for you at the point of a pistol. You could have offered me a small share and I would have been happy to help out. Hell, any trapper would be happy to lend you a hand mining this vein if you gave him enough to make it worthwhile. But no. You're too greedy. With your partner dead you want it all to yourself."

Cain took the reproach in stony silence, then said, "Who are you to lecture me, King? You trailed me all the way here just to get your horse back, to reclaim your own, and then you have the gall to blame me for wantin' to protect my own? I couldn't just go out and invite the first man I met to join me. I wouldn't know a thing about him. How could I tell if he was honest or not? Once a stranger saw the vein, once he saw how much gold there was, he just might put a knife in my back so he could have it all to himself." Cain shook his head. "Your way is for fools, or for those who are too trustin' for their own good."

Nate didn't bother debating the issue. He folded his arms and awaited further orders, but Cain wasn't done justifying himself.

"I feel bad about this, King. I truly do. After all, you did save me from Flying Hawk. And like I said before, I can see that you're an honorable . . ." Cain stopped and blinked, as if astonished by a thought. Then he glanced at the vein. "Hmmmm."

"What?"

"Maybe I'm goin' about this the wrong way. I know you'll jump me the first chance that comes along if you figure you can do it before I put a ball into Flying Hawk.

77

I'll have to be on my guard every minute. Unless . . ." Cain said, and let his voice trail off.

Nate was becoming impatient. He stared at the pistol fixed on his midsection and gauged whether he could batter it aside before Cain fired. Unfortunately, he wasn't quite close enough.

"The more I think about it, the more I like your idea," Cain suddenly declared. "I know you're a man of your word. If it means I won't have to watch my back all the time, it's worth it."

"What is?"

"Givin' you a share. You had two parfleches on your horse, as I recollect. I put 'em with the rest of my supplies. What say I let you fill 'em both with all the gold you can stuff into 'em in exchange for you agreein' to help me mine until I'm ready to cut out?"

The totally unexpected offer flabbergasted Nate. A parfleche would be able to hold 30 or 40 pounds of ore. Maybe 50. Two parfleches filled with gold wouldn't put him in the same class as John Jacob Astor by any means, but he'd have enough to tide his family over for quite a few years to come.

But was the offer sincere? Given Cain's past performance, Nate doubted it, even though the gold he'd receive was a small fraction of the total in the vein. Cain didn't just want a lion's share of the wealth; Cain wanted it all. Yet Cain was smart enough to wait until the mining was done before showing his true colors, and by then Nate would have worked out a way to put Solomon Cain in his proper place.

"What's your answer? Do you agree?" Cain prompted.

"I'm tempted," Nate confessed. "But what about Flying Hawk?"

"What about him?"

"If I agree, will you allow him to go back to his people?"

"And have him come back with a war party to take my scalp? Are you out of your mind?"

"What if I get him to give his word that he'll leave you alone?"

"I wouldn't care if he swore on his mother's grave. I still wouldn't trust him. He stays here until I'm done minin'."

"Then I can't accept your offer."

Cain made a curt gesture toward the chamber. "You'd pass up thousands in gold for some Injun? What the hell for? What's so special about him?"

"No man, white or otherwise, deserves to be treated like an animal."

Muttering under his breath, Cain began tapping his right foot. "Damn me if you ain't the most righteous son of a bitch I've ever met! You missed your callin'. You should have been a minister." He shook the flintlock as if he wanted to pound something. "I'm bein' as generous as I can and you throw it back in my face."

"Let me talk to Flying Hawk."

"No."

"Hear me out. How about if I talk him into promising not to harm you, and get his word he'll stay right here where you can keep your eyes on him until we're done mining?"

"No."

"He might listen to reason."

"No, damn it."

"Put the idea to Smoky Woman. I bet she'll agree to help us persuade him."

"You just don't understand," Cain said bitterly. "Nothin' I say or do is goin' to stop Flying Hawk from killin' me once he learns about his sister. And he will, sooner or later. She can't hide a thing like that for long."

"I don't follow you."

79

"She's carryin' my child."

Nate was so shocked he took a step backwards and nearly tripped over a chunk of quartz lying on the tunnel floor behind him. Straightening, he glanced down the passage and glimpsed Smoky Woman as she moved about in the chamber. Her condition explained a lot. No wonder she had refused to take sides when Cain and her brother clashed. And no wonder she had been so defensive about Cain.

"I want to tell you something," the father-to-be said. "It's none of your affair, but I want you to know so you won't think I'm worse than I am." He paused. "I didn't force her, King. As God is my witness, I've treated her decently since I took her. I've never beat her. Never so much as hit her."

Now Nate fully understood why Smoky Woman acted so ashamed when she was around Flying Hawk. In the eyes of her tribe she had shamed herself and her people by what she had done. Her brother, she must fear, would hate her once he learned the truth.

"Do you see the fix I'm in?" Cain asked. "I can't shoot Flying Hawk 'cause he's kin to the woman I've grown to love. And I can't let him go neither, if I want to keep on breathin'." He gestured angrily with the pistol. "You tell me. What am I supposed to do?"

"It's not for me to say," Nate replied.

"She can't go back to her people now. They'd treat her as an outcast. And they'd sure as blazes never accept me as her husband. So I have to take her away with me even though this land is her home." Cain leaned his shoulder on the wall. "I know you'll think I'm lyin', but she's the reason I hit you on the noggin when Flying Hawk and his bunch were closin' in on us. All I could think of was her, here alone with no one to depend on but me. I got scared, King. Not for me. For her. I knew the two of us on horseback would never get away from Flying Hawk,

80

but I figured I could alone. So I did what I did and I'm mighty sorry."

"I see," Nate said thoughtfully. Although he still didn't condone Cain's treachery, he felt some small sympathy for Cain's plight. There were many other trappers, himself included, who had fallen in love with Indian women, but in those instances the tribes involved were all friendly to whites. Cain had the misfortune of loving a woman whose people despised the mountain men and who might slay him for the outrage he had committed on her.

"I figure this gold will buy us the happiness we need," Cain commented, gazing fondly at the glittering vein. "We'll live in a mansion surrounded by high walls, with servants to wait on us hand and foot. I know there will be gossip, and a lot of the wealthy folks will look down their noses at us. But I don't care. We'll keep to ourselves and be perfectly happy."

"True happiness, someone once said, must come from within."

"Don't start preachin' at me again. I'm miserable enough as it is." Cain squared his shoulders and raised the flintlock. "Enough palaver. I've jawed more in the past five minutes than I have in the past five years. Give me your answer and give it to me now. Will you help me out for two parfleches of gold?"

"Yes."

"Good. You won't regret it," Cain said, wedging the pistol under his belt.

Nate touched the gold again, vaguely troubled by his decision. There was still the issue of Flying Hawk to settle. Somehow he must come up with a way of having the warrior freed. And there was one more thing. "I'll need my rifle and my flintlocks and all the rest back."

Cain visibly hesitated.

"If you don't trust me enough to hand them over, I won't help you," Nate said, facing around. This was the supreme test of Cain's sincerity. If Cain refused, Nate would know for certain the man had no intention whatsoever of ever sticking to the letter of their agreement.

"I reckon I should."

"And from here on out no one rides my horse but me."

"Anything else?" Cain asked, grinning.

"Just this," Nate said, and punched Cain flush on the jaw, his knuckles cracking hard against bone, the blow tottering Cain backwards to fall onto his back.

"What the hell!" Cain roared, scrambling up on his elbows and grabbing at a pistol.

Nate hadn't moved. "That was for the knock on the head," he explained harshly, and tensed to pounce should Cain draw the weapon.

But Cain froze, his mouth dropping open. "Well, I'll be damned!" he exclaimed, and erupted in hearty laughter, laughter that muffled the sound of approaching footsteps. Neither of them noticed Smoky Woman until she was right there, beckoning urgently.

"Come quick!" she cried. "Horses upset. Something outside!"

Chapter
Seven

Filled with fear that Pegasus would be stolen—again—
Nate raced along the tunnel and into the main chamber,
heedless of a shout from Cain urging him to stop. In
his haste and anxiety he momentarily forgot he was
unarmed. Past Flying Hawk he sprinted, then around the
bend, past the piled provisions, and out into the bright
sunshine, where he halted and glanced to his right.

Flying Hawk's horse was gone! The rest were indeed
agitated, whinnying and straining at the ropes that secured
them to nearby boulders.

Nate was afraid Pegasus would break loose. He ran
over, seized the rope in his left hand, and said, "Whoa
there! Calm down!" while patting the gelding on the
neck. Pegasus and the two other mounts, he noticed,
had their heads tilted upward and were peering intently
at the top of the rock wall. Turning, he craned his neck
and sought the cause of their fright. Barren rock was all
he saw.

"What the hell is the matter?" Cain demanded, arriving on the scene. "Where's Flying Hawk's animal?"

"I don't know," Nate said, continuing to stroke the Palouse and to scan the heights above. "Something is up there."

Cain stared at the lofty rim. "A panther, I reckon. This is the only spring for miles and critters are comin' around all the time." He pointed at hoof tracks leading to the southwest. "Its scent spooked the horses and Flying Hawk's done run off."

"Maybe," Nate acknowledged, although he had grave misgivings. Wild animals wouldn't be the only creatures drawn to the water. He saw Smoky Woman appear at the entrance and called to her. "Tell me. Do the Utes know of any tribe that lives in this barren region?"

She walked toward them, her hands clasped at her waist. "Old men say so. But no one see many, many winters. Think all dead."

"Does this tribe have a name?"

Smoky Woman spoke in Ute, caught herself, and translated slowly, choosing her words with care. "The Rock People."

What an odd name, Nate thought, although it was highly appropriate if there actually was a tribe frequenting the wasteland, which he was inclined to doubt. No one in their right mind would want to live in such a stark, lifeless domain. The way he saw it, the barefoot Indians were simply passing through the arid region on their way between the mountain range to the west and the range to the east. Naturally they would stop at the spring. He shifted to survey their general vicinity, but saw no one.

Cain addressed Smoky Woman. "Why didn't you tell me about these here Rock People?"

"You not ask."

Nate gazed westward at the setting sun, a third of which had disappeared below the far horizon. "It'll be

84

dark soon," he commented. "There's no time to go after Flying Hawk's animal now. With a panther on the prowl, we'd be smart to move our horses closer to the cave so we can keep an eye on them."

"Suit yourself," Cain said, "but you're wastin' your time. No panther is goin' to come anywhere near the spring with all the man-scent hereabouts."

Untying Pegasus, Nate led the Palouse to the entrance. A roving panther, in his opinion, was the least of their worries. More dangerous would be a return of the band that had taken Simon, and he couldn't understand why Cain wasn't more concerned over the possibility. Maybe, he mused, the sparkling allure of the gold had blinded the man to reality. Cain wanted that gold more than anything so he discounted everything that would cause a more rational man to give second thoughts to staying.

A convenient projection of rock to the right of the opening gave Nate an anchor to which he tied the gelding. One after the other he brought over the other two animals and did the same with them. While he was thus engaged, Smoky Woman took a large pan to the spring and filled it. Cain kept close to her. As they were coming back, Nate remarked, "There's not enough forage around here to feed a gopher, let alone three horses. What have you been doing?"

"Smoky Woman and me been sort of takin' turns goin' to the park every other day so they can eat their fill. She goes most of the time 'cause I'm too busy diggin' out ore. It's the best we can do under the circumstances."

After conducting a last check of the high rock wall, Nate followed the pair into the chamber. Flying Hawk had made no effort to escape in their absence; he lay on his side, slumped in dejection. Nate glanced at three rifles, one his Hawken, propped near the buffalo hide bed, and said, "I want my guns and things back now."

In short order Cain turned over the Hawken, both pistols, Nate's butcher knife and tomahawk, and showed Nate where his parfleches and other possessions had been placed. "There," Cain said. "That's all of your stuff. See? I'm holdin' up my end of the bargain."

Nate checked the flintlocks to be certain they were properly loaded. He couldn't help but wonder if Cain would still hold up his end of their pact when the time came to ride off with the gold. That was when the crucial test would come.

Smoky Woman, meanwhile, had busily gathered the items she needed to fix their supper. Now she headed back outside.

Seeing her go, Nate started to join her to serve as her protector when a hail from Cain made him turn.

"I have something to show you," Cain said. Picking up the lantern, he walked to the wall opposite from the bed. "Come over here a second," he beckoned. "What do you make of these."

Revealed in the rosy glow were numerous crude paintings depicting men and animals, but they were unlike any men or wild beasts Nate had ever beheld. The men had block-like bodies and long hair down to their waists. A few held short spears. Others held odd weapons not much bigger than their hands. Almost always the men were portrayed in the act of hunting game. In one scene a half-dozen figures had surrounded an enormous beast resembling an elephant only it had a great shaggy coat, small ears, a pair of curved tusks, and a bulge on top of its head. In another scene several men were battling a large panther-like animal sporting two top teeth exaggerated out of all proportion.

"Who could have drawn all this?" Cain wanted to know.

"Indians, maybe," Nate guessed. "Indians who lived in this cave ages ago." He based this assumption on the fact that the paint which had been used, a pigment derived from berries or perhaps from mixing water with clay as some tribes currently did, showed signs of having faded considerably.

"That's what I figured too," Cain said. "Until I saw this down here." Stepping to one side, he squatted and nodded at another painting.

In one respect the scene Cain indicated was much like the rest. It showed a group of men chasing a herd of elk. But in another respect this particular depiction was extremely unusual; the yellowish-brown streaks of paint had been applied much more recently than the rest. They almost glistened. The color was so much brighter the difference was like that between night and day.

"I'd say this was done not more than two years ago at the most," Cain mentioned. "Wouldn't you?"

"Yes," Nate agreed, feeling unduly disturbed. It was just another painting, he reasoned, yet it gave him the same sort of uneasy sensation he experienced when he encountered a grizzly and didn't know if the bear would charge or flee.

"Whoever painted it might still be around," Cain said.

"True," Nate responded, thinking of the mysterious footprints and Simon's disappearance.

Cain stepped toward the middle of the chamber. "Some of the bones don't look too old either."

"What bones?"

"That's right. I ain't taken you there yet." Cain headed into the tunnel. "Follow me and I'll show you what else we found."

They went past the exposed vein, around a curve, and along a straight passage extending for over 60 feet. Abruptly, the walls widened and they were in a second large chamber. Here fine particles of dust hung in the air. Dust caked the walls, coated the floor. And covered a mound of bones rearing over six feet high in the middle of the chamber.

Astounded, Nate stepped forward to examine them. He saw one bone he recognized immediately, the leg bone of a buffalo. A bear skull jutted from the bottom portion of the mound. On one side was the partial skeleton of a panther. None of these remains had the same effect on him as did the many human skulls that dotted the pile from top to bottom.

Human skulls! He couldn't quite accept the testimony of his own eyes. There had to be 20 or 30 he could see, and probably more buried underneath. Why, he mused, hadn't the people who lived in the cave buried their dead or else suspended them in trees or on platforms as did many Indian tribes? How uncaring to just dump the dead into this chamber with the remains of wild beasts.

Then he spied a human arm bone and he bent over for a closer look. There were odd scratches and grooves on the bone that perplexed him until he glanced at the bones of the animals and saw similar marks. Insight hit him like a bolt out of the blue. *Those were teeth marks!*

Nate snapped erect and clenched his Hawken so hard his knuckles turned white. "It can't be!" he blurted.

"It can't be, but it is," Cain said. "Took me a while to mull it over, but I figure the folks who lived here ate people as well as animals." He laughed. "Don't that beat all?"

Revolted by the images conjured up, Nate backed away from the mound. He was close to the tunnel when faintly into the chamber wafted the spine-tingling sound of a scream of mortal terror.

"Smoky Woman!" Cain bellowed.

Whirling, Nate took the lead, his legs pumping as he fairly flew along the tunnel. The scream died suddenly, filling him with gnawing dread. One of them should have gone with her. If something happened to her he was partly to blame for being so careless. Had it been Winona he would never have let her go out alone.

In the main chamber Flying Hawk was in the act of rolling frantically toward the entrance. Nate vaulted over him without breaking stride, went around the bend, and out into the murky gray of twilight.

Smoky Woman was gone.

He looked to the left and saw the horses were still there. Her scream, he figured, had forced her captors to flee before taking any of the mounts. Then he saw the pans and food scattered near the fire, showing she had put up quite a struggle.

Something made him glance at the rise. He was just in time to see several hurrying forms vanish over the crest. Wheeling, he dashed to get his saddle and nearly collided with Cain.

"Where is she? Where the hell is she?"

"They've got her."

"Oh, God!" Cain cried, advancing into the open and searching right and left. "Which way did they go? I'm goin' after 'em."

"No, I am," Nate said as he grabbed his epishimore, a square piece of blanket he used under his saddle.

"She's my woman, not yours."

"And Pegasus is my horse, not yours. He's the only chance we have of overtaking them. You've ridden him. You know how fast he is."

"I'll take him, then. You stay here in case there are more of the bastards skulkin' around."

Nate brushed past Cain and began saddling up. "You said yourself that he began giving you trouble before. He doesn't like being ridden by anyone but me."

"She's my woman, damn it!" Cain reiterated, putting his hand on Nate's shoulder. "I'm the one should go."

With a quick jerk Nate pulled loose and turned. "We don't have time to waste, Solomon. Which is more important, your pride or her life?"

Cain opened his mouth to reply, froze for a second, then changed his mind and stood aside. "You go."

In less than a minute Nate was in the saddle. "Keep the fire going so I have a beacon to guide me back here. If all goes well I won't be long."

"God go with you, King."

A gust of wind whipped by Nate as he swung the Palouse and made for the rise. His wounded shoulder ached from the exertion of throwing on the saddle, but not enough to impair his thinking, which was good because he'd need his wits about him when he caught up with the ones who'd abducted Smoky Woman.

Pegasus seemed eager for some exercise. The gelding went up the slope at a gallop, head low, mane flying.

Just over the top Nate reined up to scour the land in front of him. He didn't stop on the crest itself because he would have been silhouetted against the ever-darkening sky. Ahead lay a barren maze. Which direction should he go? He doubted the Indians had gone to the south where the land was more open since they would be more readily detected. Nor would they have gone to the north where a butte barred their path. Due east, he believed, was the right way to go.

He was sure he couldn't be more than three hundred yards behind them, if that, and consequently he pushed Pegasus at a reckless speed. Smoky Woman's abductors were bound to hear him coming, which couldn't be helped. He cocked the Hawken, set the trigger, and held the Hawken across his thighs, ready for action.

Behind him a rifle cracked.

Nate almost stopped. It was Cain who must have fired, at what he couldn't guess. Twisting, Nate listened for more shots, a sure sign the cave was under attack. But there were no more. Counting on Cain being able to hold his own, Nate galloped on into the night.

Suddenly, off to the left, a bird called. Another bird, off to the right, answered.

In all the years Nate had spent in the Rockies he had never heard birds like these. Suspicious, he looked both ways but saw only dark, bleak terrain. What if he had miscalculated? What if there were more Indians than he thought? Or were they even worthy of being called Indians? If they were related to the occupants of the cave, to the vile people who had eaten their own kind or their captives, then they didn't deserve to be dignified by the word. Savages would be more like it.

He recalled reading about the Aztecs in school. Rulers of ancient Mexico, they had built stupendous cities and been as civilized as any society that ever existed, except in one important respect. The Aztecs had indulged in ritual sacrifice and often engaged in cannibalism. Their priests would cut out and eat the hearts of those being sacrificed, while the bodies of the unfortunates would be given to the common people to be devoured at public feasts. When he'd first read the account, he'd shuddered in revulsion. Now, here he was about to tangle with a band that might be just as bad.

From out of nowhere materialized a short, stocky figure not 20 feet off. Nate glimpsed a muscular, naked body, and a wild mane of black hair. Then he glimpsed a slender object flashing toward him and realized the savage had hurled a spear. So superb were his reflexes that the instant he perceived the danger he ducked low and angled Pegasus to the right.

The spear missed them by inches.

Straightening, Nate raised the Hawken to fire but the figure was already gone. He reined up and swiveled, scanning in a circle. Now the night was quiet except for the rush of the wind, giving him the illusion he was the only soul alive in the midst of a vast alien landscape. Yet he knew better.

He also knew not to stay in one spot too long. Jabbing his heels into Pegasus, he trotted eastward once more. He touched each flintlock, insuring they were in place. So were his knife and tomahawk.

For a hundred yards the night was deceptively tranquil. He began to suspect he was going in the wrong direction and considered changing direction to the northeast or the southeast. But which should it be? Unexpected aid came in the guise of a stifled shriek to the northeast.

Hunching low over the saddle, Nate galloped across a rocky flat, the gelding's hoofs cracking like gunshots. Just when he thought he had misjudged where the shriek came from he spotted a cluster of figures straight ahead.

There were five of them, four husky, naked savages and Smoky Woman. Two of them had her in their grasp and she was striving mightily to break free. A third had his hand clamped over her mouth from behind. The fourth, trailing his companions by a few feet, heard Pegasus first and whirled.

Nate saw the man's right arm sweep back, then streak forward. But there was no spear in the man's hand, so Nate didn't slow up or turn aside. And had the savage not rushed the throw, Nate would have died then and there.

He heard a buzzing noise, as if a dozen hornets were winging past, and felt rather than saw something strike his saddle with a distinct smack. Glancing down, he was amazed to find a slender object imbedded close to his left thigh. There was no time to pull it out and inspect it, though, because seconds later he was among the savages.

Barking in a strange tongue, they scattered, one of them hauling Smoky Woman by the wrist.

Ignoring the rest, Nate snapped the Hawken to his left shoulder instead of his right, which had started acting up again after he'd slugged Cain, and sighted carefully. The

Hawken spat lead and smoke and the savage keeled over as if felled by an axe.

The moment Smoky Woman was free, she turned and ran to meet him, holding her arms up to make his next task easier.

As it was, her weight was almost too much for him with his weakened shoulder. Gripping the Hawken and the reins in his left hand, he swung low in the saddle and looped his right arm around her slim waist while at a full gallop. The shock of her body hitting his arm almost wrenched him from his perch. Had she not leaped at that precise instant, adding her momentum to the backward swing he had started, he would certainly have fallen.

As lithely as a lynx she slid up behind him and grabbed him about the waist.

There were angry shouts from several directions. Another buzzing projectile almost struck Nate's face.

Then they were out of range, riding hard, bearing to the southeast in a wide loop that would eventually take them back to the cave. Nate could feel her warm body pressed to his, reminding him of the lovely wife waiting for him in their comfortable cabin many miles away. If he had any brains, that was where he'd be instead of fleeing for his life from primitive Indians who'd enjoy having him for their evening meal. Literally.

Once he believed they had left the savages far behind, he slowed to a walk to reduce the amount of noise Pegasus was making. For all he knew, other bands might be abroad and he wanted to avoid them if at all possible.

"Thank you," Smoky Woman whispered at length.

"You're welcome," Nate whispered in reply.

"Cain?"

"He's fine. Mad as a bee in a bonnet, but fine. He wanted to come after you himself but I talked him out of it."

"Why?"

Nate explained about Pegasus's finicky nature.

"My brother?"

"He's fine too," Nate assured her, mentally noting that she'd asked after Cain first. He added, "I sure do hope the two of you will be back on friendly terms soon. Brothers and sisters have a special blood bond between them. They should always try to love each other."

"My brother not love me again."

"He'll come around. Men can be stubborn cusses, but we see the light sooner or later."

"See light?"

"Yes. We learn not to be so stubborn."

"My brother never see light."

"Don't be so hard on him. He might surprise you."

"I know him."

"Have you told him about the baby yet?" Nate inquired, and felt her arms briefly constrict on his midsection.

"How you know?"

"Cain told me."

Smoky Woman fell silent. Nate assumed she was upset he knew. Perhaps she viewed her pregnancy as highly personal and no business of anyone else except Cain and her.

The wind had died. Stygian gloom shrouded the wasteland, relieved only by a quarter moon and the myriad of shining stars. From the southwest came the lonesome yip of a solitary coyote.

Nate reloaded the Hawken as he rode. He had to measure the amount of black powder by the feel of the grains in the palm of his hand, which was always a tricky proposition. If he put in too little his next shot would lack the usual wallop and might fail to down an attacker at a critical instant. If he put in too much he risked bursting the percussion tube of his rifle. But he had reloaded by feel so many times he was confident he put in just the right amount.

His nerves on edge, the stock of the Hawken resting on his left thigh, he searched for some sign of the blazing fire. It should be easy to spot, yet over the course of the next 40 minutes the blanket of darkness lay unbroken on the land. Had Cain neglected to keep the fire going? he wondered. Or was there a more sinister reason for its absence?

He grew certain they were near the high rock wall. Stopping, he listened and looked. To his right was the familiar rise. A black patch was all that could be seen of the cave. He couldn't even tell if the other horses were still there.

Goading Pegasus forward, Nate leveled the Hawken in case the savages lurked nearby. He was within 20 yards of the entrance when a rifle boomed and the ball whizzed past his ear.

Chapter
Eight

Since, in Nate's estimation, none of the savages possessed guns and they wouldn't know how to use a pistol or a rifle if they had it, only one person could have fired at him. "Cain! You idiot! It's King! Don't shoot!"

A yelp of joy greeted his shout. "Sorry! I thought you were one of those devils! Come on in!"

Smoky Woman's grip slackened as they neared the entrance, and Pegasus had barely stopped when she jumped off and ran into the outstretched arms of Solomon Cain.

Nate was dismounting when another figure strode from the cave. "Flying Hawk!" he declared in surprise, for not only was the warrior free but Cain had even given back the Ute's bow, arrows, and hunting knife.

"Let's get under cover and I'll fill you in," Cain said, motioning for Nate to go first. "We took the other horses inside so the bastards can't steal 'em."

The animals were between the entrance and the bend. Nate tied Pegasus in the feeble light from a single candle placed so as not to be visible beyond the opening. As he did his gaze fell on the slender object imbedded in his saddle. He had to wrench hard to pluck it out.

It was unlike any weapon Nate had ever heard of. The only thing he could compare it to were the darts used in popular games played in taverns back in the States. This dart was made of stone and had two slim raven feathers tied to a groove at the back end to add stability in flight. Simple, but extremely deadly.

"What have you got there?" Cain asked, walking over. He whistled softly. "So that's what some of the sons of bitches were throwin'! I heard a couple go by me and one nicked my sleeve."

"And I heard your shot. What happened?"

"You weren't gone very long when I spotted a pack of savages sneakin' up on me from the west. I let 'em get close, and when one jumped up and went to toss a spear I shot him smack between the eyes. Some of the others tried to nail me but I made it in here. Had to kick out the fire on my way, which made me a good target. But they didn't want to get too close. Guess they were afraid of the rifle." Cain paused to smile at Smoky Woman. "While I reloaded I could see 'em movin' around out there. That set me to thinkin'. If they rushed me all at once, I wouldn't stand a prayer. So I did the only thing I could. I ran on back and told Flying Hawk I'd free him if he'd help us. He agreed, but only till his sister is out of danger."

And then what? Nate reflected. Once Smoky Woman was safe, what would Flying Hawk do? Kill Cain? The warrior was at the entrance, keeping watch.

"He was the one thought of bringin' in the horses," Cain commented. "Smart move too."

"Have the savages attacked yet?"

"Nope. They were flittin' around like butterflies until a few minutes ago. I figure they heard you comin' and lit out."

"They won't give up so easily," Nate said, tucking the dart under his belt next to a pistol. Hurrying to the Ute, he signed, "See anything?"

Flying Hawk grunted and pointed.

At the limits of human vision ghostly forms were gliding about like wolves around trapped prey, moving from one place of concealment to another. Sometimes two or three would meet, confer, and separate.

"Are they still there?" Cain asked.

"Yes. They must have let Smoky Woman and me through their lines so they'd have us all boxed in together."

"Damn their hides."

Nate heartily concurred. Primitive they might be, but the savages weren't stupid. He must not make the mistake of underestimating them.

"I say we make a break for it," Cain declared. "Load up the gold on the three horses and head out before the bastards charge us. We'll be on foot, but it's so dark they might miss."

"Might," Nate said, conjuring up a vision of what a hail of darts and spears would do to them and the horses. "But there are so many out there now that the odds are we'd never get fifty feet."

"I'm willin' to chance it if you are."

"The only way we'd make it is if we left the gold behind," Nate mentioned. "On foot, leading the horses, we wouldn't stand a prayer." He looked at Solomon. "Even if we leave the gold, one of us will have to ride double with Smoky Woman. The horse would take longer crossing the flat to the wash, and we both know what that would mean. Do you still want to chance it?"

"No," Cain answered, gazing affectionately at the woman. "No, I reckon I don't. And I sure ain't leavin' the gold."

"Then I suggest we make a barricade using the supplies and the packs of gold."

"The gold!" Cain exclaimed. "Not on your life. I want it in the chamber where it's safe and sound!"

"Those packs are the heaviest things in the whole cave. We can put them on the bottom as the foundation for our barricade," Nate said. "We have nothing else to use in their place."

Clearly Cain hated the idea. His face scrunched up as if he'd just swallowed a mouthful of bitterroot. "All right," he spat. "You've convinced me."

Flying Hawk stood guard while Nate, Cain, and Smoky Woman worked swiftly. Fifteen minutes of industrious labor produced a makeshift wall three feet high and extending two-thirds of the way across the cave opening. Standing back to inspect their handiwork, Nate shook his head in disappointment. The barricade was too flimsy and incomplete to hold out a concerted rush for very long. But it was the best they could do.

Cain must have entertained the same thoughts because he said, "We can use my shovels to scoop out a wall of dirt to finish it off."

And that's what they did, or started to, when Flying Hawk spoke a word of warning and jabbed a finger to the south.

The ghostly forms were converging on the cave.

No words were necessary. Nate retrieved his Hawken and crouched near the gap between their barricade and the east wall, the most vulnerable spot. "Make every shot count," he said softly.

Cain ran to the flickering candle and extinguished the flame with his thumb and forefinger. Then he took up

David Thompson

a post close to Nate. To Cain's right was Flying Hawk. Behind them, clutching a pair of flintlocks Cain had taught her to use, squatted Smoky Woman.

Smiling grimly, Flying Hawk notched an arrow to his bow string.

"Wait until I give the signal," Nate said, and heard Cain repeat it in the Ute tongue. Their breathing was the only sound after that. Oddly, the savages weren't making any noise as they charged, unlike typical Indians, who invariably whooped when engaged in a battle.

"King?" Cain whispered.

"What?"

"If something should happen to me, don't let these bastards get their hands on Smoky Woman. We both know what they'll do to her. Promise me you'll take care of it."

"I promise," Nate said, hoping he wouldn't have to. But if the worst did occur, he wasn't going to let them take him alive either.

By now the savages were 30 feet off. Strung out in an uneven line, they bounded forward like a pack of hungry wolves, their manes of black hair blowing in the breeze. Some were armed with spears, some with war clubs, some with their unusual darts.

Taking a steady bead on one of the foremost runners, Nate held his breath, cried, "Now!" and fired. Cain's rifle also cracked, followed a second later by the twang of Flying Hawk's powerful bow.

There was no time to reload the Hawken. Nate set it down, drew both pistols, and extended his arms. The initial volley had caused some of the savages to slow, but the undaunted majority were still closing. He aimed at one and squeezed off his shot, aimed at another and emptied the second flintlock. Cain was also shooting. Four or five of the savages were down, several thrashing in agony.

Nate discarded the pistol and yanked out both his knife and his tomahawk. This was the moment of truth. Fully a half-dozen savages would reach the barricade in the next few seconds.

The bowstring twanged, reducing the number to five.

A burly Indian bearing an upraised club hurled himself at the gap and Nate moved to meet him. Nate blocked the downward sweep of the savage's club with the tomahawk, then speared his butcher knife into his foe's chest.

The man roared and jerked backwards, tearing the knife out. Heedless of the hole and his spurting blood, the Indian snapped the club up and sprang.

Nate deftly blocked the blow with the tomahawk, then lashed his knife in a tight arc, going for the savage's throat this time. Nimble as a bighorn, the Indian swerved, shifted, and slammed his club into Nate's side. Incredible pain sheared through Nate's chest. For a desperate moment he thought his ribs had caved in. Doubled over in torment, he glanced up to see the savage raising the club for the death stroke, and with a sinking feeling in his gut he knew he lacked the strength to dodge.

An arrow abruptly skewered the burly Indian's throat, sinking in almost to the eagle feather fletching. Driven rearward by the impact, the savage grasped the shaft and snapped it off as easily as Nate might snap a mere twig. Furious, seemingly unfazed, the man took a step and prepared to bash Nate's skull in. A second arrow, however, transfixed the Indian's chest, and he toppled where he stood.

Nate finally straightened, intending to thank Flying Hawk, but another savage had already taken the place of the first. This one carried a spear that he slashed at Nate's face. Nate pivoted, the spear fanned his nose, and with a mighty surge of all the muscles in his left shoulder he sank his tomahawk into his enemy's forehead. Like an

David Thompson

overripe melon the brow split right down the middle, the keen blade cleaving the brain. Instantly the savage went into violent convulsions, nearly tearing the tomahawk from Nate's grasp before he could rip it loose.

Nate turned, expecting more adversaries, finding none. Five bodies lay sprawled over or near the partially crumbled barricade, while the rest of the primitive Indians were retreating into the impenetrable cover of the night. Elated, he leaned on a parfleche in front of him, but only for a heartbeat. The savages, he realized, might regroup and mount another attack. Sliding the tomahawk under his belt and the knife into its sheath, he gathered up his guns to reload them. A groan made him look to his right.

Cain was braced against the back wall, a slain savage at his feet, a bloody knife in his right hand. His left shoulder sagged as if under a tremendous weight, and he swayed when he took a step away from the wall. In a flash Smoky Woman was at his side, supporting him.

"What happened?" Nate asked as he pulled the Hawken's ramrod out. "How bad is it?"

"Took a damn club in the shoulder," Cain answered, his lips drawn back in a grimace. "I think the bone is busted."

"Sit down and rest. I'll be with you in a bit," Nate said. With Cain temporarily indisposed, his first priority was to reload all their guns, not just his own, or they'd never survive another onslaught. Flying Hawk, he observed, was staring intently at Smoky Woman.

"I can manage," Cain said, stepping to the barricade. He leaned over to pick up his rifle, then groaned louder than before and slowly sank to his knees. "Hurts like hell!" he declared. "Almost blacked out there."

"Hold on," Nate urged, his fingers moving quickly. They needed Cain badly. Smoky Woman could shoot, but she was nowhere near the marksman Cain was.

Without him they would drop fewer savages when the next rush came, meaning more would reach the barricade and possibly overwhelm them by sheer force of numbers.

An unnerving silence now claimed the countryside. Nothing moved. The erratic wind had subsided to a whisper.

Relying on Flying Hawk to warn him if the savages reappeared, Nate concentrated exclusively on feeding black powder and balls into gun after gun. Soon he had all the rifles and pistols reloaded. His flintlocks once again under his belt, he dropped to one knee beside Solomon Cain, who sat slumped against the barricade. "Is the pain still bad?"

"I feel like a grizzly clamped its jaws down on my shoulder and won't let go."

"Let me take a look," Nate said, gingerly touching the wounded shoulder.

Cain flinched, then hissed as if angry at himself and sat up straight. "I'm gettin' right puny of late. Must be all this soft livin'." He mustered a wan grin.

"I'll try not to hurt you," Nate said, but it was unavoidable. Twice he made Cain gasp as he probed carefully to measure the extent of the damage. One gasp came when he touched a bone that moved when it shouldn't. "You were right," he said after he was done. "Your clavicle is broken."

"My what?"

"Your shoulder bone."

"Of all the stinkin' luck," Cain muttered.

"I can try to set the bone and bandage you up. It won't be as good as a sawbones would do, but it'll hold you together if you don't go out and wrestle any wolverines."

Cain gazed at Smoky Woman. "Forget me. Those bastards may try again. You need to keep watch so they don't catch us by surprise."

103

"Your skin is split open. The longer we wait, the more chance of infection setting in," Nate said. He nodded at the barricade. "We might wind up being penned in here for a long time. If you get sick, we won't be able to give you the doctoring you'll need. So don't be mule-headed. Allow me to do what I can now and save us a lot of trouble later."

"If you put it that way," Cain said.

"I do." Nate slipped an arm around Cain's waist and helped him to rise. "Have Smoky Woman take you back into the main chamber. See if she can somehow get a fire going. I'll need hot water if I'm to do this right."

"All right." Cain chuckled. "You sure have a knack for givin' orders. Forget bein' a minister. Join the army and you'll be a general in no time."

Nate leaned his forearms on the top of the barricade and scanned the land fronting the entrance. The savages had yet to show themselves. Could it be that they had departed? They'd suffered heavy losses, undoubtedly more than they had expected. Would they risk as many lives in another attack? Or would they do as the Apaches often did when the Apaches met stiffer resistance than they anticipated, cut their losses and go in search of easier pickings? Suddenly a finger touched his shoulder.

Flying Hawk moved his hands in exaggerated movements so the signs he made would be conspicuous in the dark. "You are a fine fighter, Grizzly Killer. I no longer doubt you are worthy of your name."

"Thank you," Nate signed in the same exaggerated manner.

"Do you know the secret my sister is keeping from me?"

The blunt query caught Nate flat-footed and he paused before responding, uncertain whether he should reveal the truth or deny he knew anything. He loathed lying, but by the same token he didn't have the right to meddle in Smoky Woman's personal affairs. She must have an excellent reason for not informing her brother.

"Do not try to deny she is hiding something," Flying Hawk signed. "I know her well, Grizzly Killer, as well as I do myself. She can hide nothing from me for very long."

"If she does have a secret," Nate signed tactfully, "it is for her to tell you. I would be out of place were I to give it away."

The warrior did not respond immediately. His features obscured by shadow, he stood as still as if carved from stone. Finally his hands moved. "Very well. I will respect your wishes." Shifting, he glanced toward the bend. "But I already think I know what her secret is, and if I am right I must take steps to prevent her from staining our family and our people."

Nate straightened. "You cannot mean that. She is your own flesh and blood."

"If what I suspect is true, she should have killed herself rather than lie with him."

"Maybe she loves him. Have you thought of that?"

"Love is no excuse for lying with an enemy."

"You disappoint me, Flying Hawk. I thought you had come to see that not all whites are as bad as some of your people might claim."

"I have. By knowing you I have learned there are white men who are brave and truthful, but this does not change anything. It does not change what has happened and what will happen. Already have your kind killed most of the beaver. One day your people will want these mountains for their own. You said so yourself. Do friends take that which does not belong to them? No. This is an act of an enemy. So whether you like it or not, your people and mine are enemies."

Nate knew there was nothing he could say to change the warrior's mind. Flying Hawk's logic was irrefutable, and were he in the Ute's place he'd feel the same way.

"If my people were to find out my sister has slept with a white man, they would shun her. The child would be treated even worse. Do not look at me like that. I have heard that your people do not think highly of mixed unions either."

"Some do not," Nate admitted, and would have gone on to appeal to the warrior's sense of fairness if not for the untimely arrival of Smoky Woman.

"Have fire. Need water." She held out a pot. "I fetch."

"Not on your life," Nate said, snatching it from her hand and moving quickly to the end of the barricade to forestall any protest. Hunching down and staying close to the cliff, he trotted toward the spring. Not until he had covered over ten feet did the gravity of the risk he was taking sink home. And all for a man he didn't like all that much.

No, he told himself. That wasn't quite true. He wasn't doing this for Cain so much as he was for Smoky Woman. For her he felt acute sympathy, and he wished there was something he could do to lessen her misery. There wasn't, though. She had made the difficult choice and she must now live with the inevitable consequence.

The smooth surface of the pool reflected the stars overhead, a glimmering mirror afloat in a dull sea of rock and packed earth, easy for him to distinguish. He halted a dozen feet off and crouched. Slowly, his mind cautioned. To rush now would prove fatal. There had to be savages nearby, and perhaps one or two were keeping an eye on the spring.

Of a sudden the wind picked up again, cooling his cheeks and brow. He ran his eyes over every boulder, every shadow. Any savages in hiding were invisible.

Easing onto his stomach, the Hawken in his left hand, the pot in his right, he snaked toward the pool, advancing an inch at a time, moving first one limb, then another, much like an oversized turtle moving in slow motion. He had to be extra careful not to scrape the rifle or the pot on the ground. Once he slipped up and the pot made a scratching noise. Freezing, he waited to see if there would be a reaction. The night mocked his anxiety with its tranquility.

At the water's edge he inhaled the dank scent and touched his fingers to the cool surface. Cupping his right hand, he ladled water to his mouth and drank quietly. Then he slowly lowered the pot in. Water flowed over the sides, filling it rapidly, making it heavier and harder to hold.

Somewhere to the west arose a faint clattering.

Nate lifted the pot out and set it down to free both hands for using the Hawken. The clattering stopped before he could identify it. Staying motionless, he fixed his eyes blankly on the entire scene before him rather than on any one specific spot. It was an old trick used to detect the slightest movement anywhere within one's view.

Over a minute must have gone by when a light-colored apparition materialized to the southwest. Assuming it must be a savage, he tucked the Hawken to his shoulder and leveled the rifle across the pool, the barrel so close to the surface it was nearly touching. Gradually the apparition solidified, transforming into a small doe, not much over a year old. Demonstrating the age-old vigilance of her species, she would take several steps, then pause to test the wind.

Nate knew the animal was coming to drink. In order to avoid giving her a scare and having her bound off, making all kinds of noise as she fled, he backed away from the pool, taking the pot in his right hand. He had gone a yard or so when he saw the most remarkable sight.

From four directions at once sprang four husky savages, swooping down on the startled doe in a blur of lightning speed. She bounded to the left, saw a savage bearing down on her, and reversed direction, bounding to the right. Another savage blocked her escape route. Spinning, she sought to flee the way she had come but another savage was there. They had her completely hemmed in. Game to the last, she darted between two of them, or tried to, but they were amazingly fast. One got her by the neck, the other dived and grabbed her front legs, and she bleated in terror as she went down.

Nate distinctly heard a loud snap.

The four savages huddled around their kill, tearing at her with their hands. One of them, exhibiting superhuman strength, tore off her hind leg and commenced greedily devouring her raw flesh. Another leaned down to rip into her slender neck with his teeth.

Nate had seen enough. Now, while they were distracted, was the perfect time to head for the cave. Turning, he crawled but three or four inches when he saw another savage, this one standing at the base of the cliff wall between the pool and the cave. And the man was coming toward him!

Chapter
Nine

Nate had the Hawken up and aimed in the blink of an eye, and he was all set to cock the hammer when he realized the savage was *backing* toward him. The man hadn't seen him yet. He surmised the Indian had snuck close to the cave entrance, perhaps to see or overhear what was going on inside, and now was sneaking off to make a report to the rest of the band. Lowering the Hawken, he drew his tomahawk. Stealth and silence were in order. Should those eating the deer hear a commotion, they would be on him before he could reach safety.

He marveled at how quiet the savage was. Strain his ears as he might, he heard nary a whisper of sound. Nate held the tomahawk flat in front of him and smelled the odor of drying blood. There had been no time to wipe the tomahawk clean after the battle, and he certainly couldn't do so now.

Suddenly the savage turned away from the cliff, bent at the waist, and sprinted off to the south, his gaze on the cave the whole time. Soon the night swallowed him up.

Nate felt some of the tension drain from his body. That had been too close for his liking! How lucky the man had been more intent on not being spotted by someone within the cave than on his surroundings! Tucking the tomahawk back under his belt, Nate gripped the rifle and the pot and resumed crawling.

From the look of things, the savages intended to stay there for a while. They were more persistent than Nate had imagined. And when he regarded the situation from their perspective, he realized they had everything to gain and little to lose by waiting around. Eventually he and the others would run out of food, and they would run out of water too if the savages thought to keep a closer watch on the spring.

Nearing the barricade, Nate whispered, "It's me!" so Flying Hawk wouldn't put an arrow into him. Then, rising, he ran the remaining distance and sank low behind the barricade with water sloshing over the rim of the pot.

The Ute and his sister were also hunched low, glaring at one another. Evidently they'd had another argument. Neither moved for fully half a minute, until Smoky Woman turned, took the pot without speaking, and hurried off, carefully holding the pot so she wouldn't spill it.

Nate leaned the Hawken against the barricade and rose high enough to peer over the top. Someone had to keep watch, and Flying Hawk was too preoccupied. Nothing moved out there. Craning his neck, Nate tried to catch a glimpse of the four savages consuming the doe, but they were too far off. A hand touched his right shoulder.

The warrior had moved closer and now employed sign, holding his hands close to Nate's face so Nate would have no problem reading the gestures.

Nate concentrated so he wouldn't miss a one. From long practice he mentally filled in the articles and other words that were lacking in sign language but which were needed to flesh out the statements into their English equivalent. In this instance Flying Hawk signed, "Sister want go white country with False Tongue. Question. Whites make her heart bad."

Sign language, incorporating as it did hundreds of hand gestures and motions, could convey a nearly endless variety of meanings and sentiments through the proper combination of symbols. But there were deficiencies, one being that in sign there were no gestures for "what," "where," "when," and "why." The sign for "question" was used instead. So when someone wanted to ask, "What are you called?" they would sign, "Question you called."

There were others areas in which sign language was lacking, from an English language standpoint, and some trappers had difficulty in reading and using sign because of this. They were accustomed to structuring their talk in a certain way and they couldn't get the hang of doing it differently. Others, like Shakespeare McNair, were as adept as the Indians themselves.

Nate raised his arms and replied. "Your sister will be treated kindly by some, not so kindly by others."

"She should stay with her own people. I do not like this."

"It might be for the best," Nate said, although he wasn't entirely convinced that it would be. Half-breeds were not highly regarded in either culture. Whites tended to treat breeds with contempt, while the attitude of the Indians varied from tribe to tribe. The Shoshones and Apaches accepted them; the Utes and Blackfeet did not.

"I will not let her go."

"She is a grown woman. She can do as she pleases."

"That is the white way, not ours."

111

"Should you stand in her way if her love for False Tongue brings her happiness?"

"She must not be permitted to shame our family and dishonor our people."

Sighing, Nate let the subject drop. It was a hopeless case, he reflected. The warrior's prejudices were too ingrained. He suddenly recalled he had promised to tend Cain's wound. "Keep watch," he signed. "If they attack again give a shout."

Tendrils of acrid smoke performed aerial dances in the main chamber. Although Smoky Woman had intentionally kept her fire small, the lack of ventilation was causing the smoke to accumulate swiftly. Steam rose off the water in the pot, giving the air a muggy feel.

Solomon Cain was on his back on a thick buffalo robe. He looked up at Nate and asked, "Are the sons of bitches still out there?"

Nate nodded. "And I suspect they have no intention of leaving any time soon. They might try to starve us out."

"I'm not about to sit in here until I'm too weak from hunger to lift my guns. We'll make a break for it come first light."

"I thought you'd decided against that notion."

Cain shifted to make himself more comfortable. "A man can change his mind, can't he? I've been lyin' here thinkin', and I have me a plan."

"Let's hear it."

"You let Smoky Woman ride double with you. Your horse is the best of the bunch, and even with her on board it'll do right fine. Until we hit cover I'll ride on one side of you and Flying Hawk will ride on the other. Between us we'll keep those pesky devils off your back."

"That's your plan?"

"Do you have a better one?" Cain said gruffly. "We sure as hell can't stay in here and rot. Sure, we might

112

be able to hold out for a spell, but think of the horses. They can't go for long without food and water. We have to cut out, if only for their sake." Cain paused. "Unless you want to try and reach the mountains on foot."

No, Nate most definitely didn't. Kneeling, he placed the Hawken at his side and did some calculations. On foot, during the daylight hours, it would take them six hours or better to get to the eastern range, six hours of grueling travel over hot terrain with the savages dogging then every step of the way. If they went at night the journey would take even longer, but the blistering heat wouldn't be a factor.

"What do you say?" Cain prompted.

"Let's wait and see how things go," Nate hedged, bending over. "Right now we have to get your shirt off."

"Use your knife. I ain't about to try liftin' my arm."

The blade sliced into the buckskin garment easily enough. Nate started at the elbow and sliced upward, using exquisite care so as not to cut Cain. Once he had a slit from Cain's elbow to Cain's neck, he peeled back the buckskin for a closer examination. In the flickering light of the candles he saw a nasty gash, over an inch deep, above the clavicle. Blood still trickled out.

"Ain't a pretty sight, is it?" Cain asked.

"I've seen worse."

"In a way Providence was lookin' out for my hide. The vermin who did this was tryin' to bash in my head. Nearly caught me by surprise." Cain grunted when Nate touched the gash. "Go easy there, hoss. This coon ain't been in such pain since the time I tangled with a grizzly near the Green River. He came chargin' out of the brush and took a swat at me. Just one, mind you. That was enough to send me flyin' over twenty feet. About stove in all my ribs, he did."

Nate glanced at Smoky Woman. "Is the water boiling yet?"

"No."

"Let me know when it is," Nate said, and cast about for something to make bandages from. Everything except the buffalo hide and Cain's possibles bag had been taken out to use in building the barricade. "What do you have in there?" he asked, nodding at the big leather bag.

"The usual. My pipe and kinnikinnick, some sewing needles, a spool of thread, pemmican and whatnot. Why?"

Nate told him.

"I got me a white Hudson's bay blanket in my supplies. A three-pointer. Best blanket I ever owned, but it won't do me no good if I'm gone beaver. Look for a parfleche with a bunch of blue beads on the front in the shape of a raven's head. It's stuffed in there."

"I'll be right back," Nate said, and went to the barricade. Flying Hawk was now standing, leaning against the wall at the point where the barricade began. The Ute offered no comment as Nate searched until he found Cain's parfleche. Pulling out the heavy blanket, he hurried back.

By then the water was boiling vigorously. Nate cut off a towel-sized piece of blanket, partially filled a tin cup with scalding water, and squatted next to Solomon Cain. "I don't need to tell you this will hurt like the dickens."

"At least it ain't an arrow in the hump-ribs."

Cutting another, smaller, square off the Hudson's bay blanket, Nate gave it to Cain. "Something to clamp down on," he advised.

"You're right considerate."

First Nate had to wash the wound thoroughly. He did this by dipping the improvised towel in the tin cup, then applying the blanket to the gash. Cain's eyes bulged and

114

he uttered intermittent gurgling noises. The water in the cup became red with blood and Nate refilled it. Presently he had the wound clean, so he put the cup down. "I going to try and set the bone," he announced.

Cain merely grunted.

The task wasn't for the squeamish. Nate had to slide two of his fingers into the gash until he touched the sagging broken bone, which he then tugged upward until he felt it make contact with the other half. His skin crawled when he felt the two sections grate together.

Beads of perspiration dotted Cain's forehead and his hair hung limp and damp. Twice he arched his spine and turned the color of a setting sun. When the sections of bone touched he let out a strangled cry, his eyelids quivering, then slumped back, barely conscious.

Nate extracted his fingers and wiped them on his leggins. Next he cut four long, wide strips off the blanket. As he began to apply one to Cain's shoulder, Smoky Woman came over.

"Let me."

The eloquent appeal in her eyes convinced Nate to relinquish the strips. Cradling the Hawken in the crook of his elbow, he walked around the bend. Pegasus nudged him, trying to get his attention, but he walked on to the barricade. "False Tongue will be fine before a moon has passed," he signed.

Flying Hawk scowled. "It would have been better had he been killed. My sister would not abandon her people then."

"And what about her baby? Do you want her to raise the child by herself?"

"There will be no baby."

The vehemence with which the warrior gestured alarmed Nate. "You would not harm an infant?"

"There will be no baby," Flying Hawk reiterated, and turned away to stare out into the night.

Deeply disturbed, Nate walked to the horses and pretended to be interested in the Palouse while his mind whirled with the dreadful implication of the Ute's statement. Should he warn Cain and Smoky Woman or keep his mouth shut? The squabble was none of his affair but he couldn't stand by and do nothing, not with the life of an innocent at stake.

During the next hour nothing of note transpired. Nate checked on Cain and found him slumbering peacefully, Smoky Woman sitting at his side. Flying Hawk appeared to be in a foul mood so Nate left him alone.

As more time elapsed and the savages failed to attack, Nate knew his guess about their strategy had been accurate. The Indians were going to starve then out. He made a check of the food and figured there was enough to last then for a week if they ate sparingly. But, as Cain had pointed out, there was no feed for the horses.

The harrowing events of the day and night took their toll. Nate's eyelids became leaden. He made bold to approach Flying Hawk and suggested they take turns keeping watch in order for each of then to catch some sleep. The Ute agreed and volunteered to stand guard first.

Spreading his blanket near the horses, Nate reclined on his back, his head propped in his hands, and stared at the inky ceiling. Sometimes he had to wonder what could have possessed him to venture into the brutal heart of the untamed wilderness when back in New York City he could have lived in perfect safety and comfort! His Uncle Zeke had been the one who enticed his by implying he would acquire the greatest treasure a man could own. And off he'd gone, mistakenly believing Zeke was referring to gold, when all the time Zeke had been talking about an entirely different and greater treasure, the priceless gift of untrammeled freedom.

Was true freedom worth all he went through simply to stay alive? The question itself was ridiculous. He remembered life in New York City, with countless thousands scurrying to and from work each day, toiling ceaselessly to make ends meet, to put food on the table and keep a roof over their heads. Yes, they lived in safety and relative comfort, but at what price? They were slaves to the money they earned, caught in a vicious circle from which there was no escape unless by some miracle they should become rich, in which case they would hoard their wealth like squirrels hoarded pine cones and nuts, as miserly with their riches as they had been in their poverty.

He started to yawn, and suppressed it lest he make a sound. Closing his eyes, he envisioned his wife's beautiful face floating in the air above him, and he wondered if he would ever see that face again.

Sleep abruptly claimed him.

The light touch of something on his shoulder brought Nate up with a start. His hand closed on the Hawken as he blinked and looked around to see Flying Hawk beside him.

"Your time," the Ute signed.

"Oh," Nate mumbled in English. He shook his head to clear lingering cobwebs, then stood and motioned for Flying Hawk to use his blanket. After a moment's hesitation the warrior accepted the offer.

By the position of the few stars Nate could see from behind the barricade, he estimated the time to be close to four in the morning. Flying Hawk had stood guard for more than half the night. Settling down where he commanded a clear view of the area outside, Nate leaned the Hawken within easy reach.

Soon dawn would break. The temperature would climb steadily until by noon they would be sweltering even

117

in the cave. Without water they would be parched by sundown.

Idly glancing to his left, he was surprised to see the dead savages had been piled in the gap between the barricade and the far wall, effectively blocking off the opening. Flying Hawk had been busy during the night.

As he stared at the corpses his memory was jogged. Somewhere, sometime, he'd heard something about Indians who were just like or very similar to these. But where? Then he recollected the Rendezvous of '27. Or was it '28? In any event, he'd been seated around a campfire with nine or ten other men listening to Jim Bridger relate various adventures.

At one point Bridger told one of his favorite stories, about the time back in '24 when he and a group of friends took to arguing over how far Bear River went. Bets were wagered. Bridger was picked to go find out. He shot a buffalo and stretched the skin hide over a framework of willow branches to make a bullboat. Then off he went.

Mile after mile Bridger followed the river until he came to a huge body of water no white man had ever laid eyes on before. When he dipped his hand in he was astonished to find the water was salty. Bridger had just discovered Big Salt Lake, as the trappers usually referred to it.

During the course of this story Bridger had talked about various Indian tribes inhabiting the region, and then repeated a story told to him by a Snake warrior. West of the Salt Lake, the Snake had claimed, lived a tribe known as the Root Eaters, or Digger Indians, who went around stark naked and lived on roots, seeds, fish, frogs, and whatever else they could find. Some of them were supposed to be as hairy as bears. The Snake had spoken of then with contempt, comparing them to animals.

Were these the same tribe? Or another just like the Diggers? Bridger had not mentioned anything about the Root Eaters having a taste for human flesh, as the bones in the back chamber indicated these did. Perhaps, Nate reasoned, his imagination was getting the better of him. Perhaps these Indians didn't eat captives. Nonetheless, they were extremely dangerous.

Shortly the sky grew progressively lighter. The stars faded by gradual degrees. A pink and orange tinge painted the eastern horizon and transformed the snowcaps on the regal peaks into crowns of radiant glory.

Nate stretched and rubbed his eyes. He could use ten or twelve hours of undisturbed sleep, a luxury he was unlikely to enjoy for quite some time. Since he had taken over the watch there had been no sign of the savages, but as sure as he was breathing he knew they were lurking out there, hidden, just waiting their chance.

The soft patter of feet made him turn.

"Good morning," Smoky Woman said softly.

"How's Cain doing?" Nate inquired.

"Very weak. Very hot. Skin burn."

"Do you still have some of the water left?"

"Yes," Smoky Woman answered, and held up her hand, her thumb and forefinger extended and several inches apart. "This much."

Which wasn't much at all, Nate reflected dourly. Before noon they must decide whether to make a dash for the spring or to suffer through the whole day and try after dark. Given Cain's condition, they could ill afford to wait that long.

"I forget thank you what you do last night," Smoky Woman said."

"I did what I had to."

"You not like him?"

Rather than hurt her feelings by being frank, Nate said, "I've met more trustworthy folks in my time."

"Cain good man."

Only a fool disputed with a woman in love over the object of her affections, and Nate was no fool. "I hope you're right, for your sake," was all he said.

An uncomfortable silence descended. Nate, aware he was wasting his time, occupied himself by scanning their vicinity for concealed savages.

"You like pemmican or jerky for breakfast?" Smoky Woman inquired.

"Jerky will do me fine," Nate said, his gaze on her until she rounded the turn. He saw Flying Hawk's eyes snap open and suspected the warrior had been awake for some time. "Morning," he said with a smile.

Flying Hawk gave a curt nod and slowly stood. The quiver went across his back. The powerful bow was held in his brawny left hand as he stepped to the barricade and peered out.

"All has been quiet," Nate signed.

As if to prove Nate wrong, a lone savage 40 yards out darted from one boulder to another, his body a blur. One moment he was there, the next he wasn't. If not for a tiny swirl of dust the man made, Nate would have doubted his eyes.

Flying Hawk had whipped up the bow, but the savage was under cover before he could nock a shaft.

"I wonder how many more are out there," Nate mused aloud. He'd seen five last night, but there might be many times that number. When the time came to try for the spring he'd probably find out exactly how many there were.

That time came sooner than anticipated. An hour and a half later, with the heat rising steadily, Smoky Woman came to Nate and said urgently, "Come see. Cain very bad."

One look at the sweat glistening on Cain's feverish brow, listening to Cain mutter incoherently as he tossed and turned on the buffalo hide, was enough to persuade Nate they must obtain fresh water immediately since the pot was almost empty. Smoky Woman had been draping wet cloths on Cain's brow and neck to keep his temperature down. Since they couldn't exactly stroll out to the spring and back, they'd need a better container than the pot to hold the water or risk spilling most of it along the way. "Does Cain own a water bag?" he inquired.

"I think yes," Smoky Woman responded. "I see." Spinning, she scurried off.

Nate stayed with Cain, sopping sweat off the man's face, until she came back bearing an old, empty water bag made from a buffalo bladder. It had not seen use in quite a spell. He would have to remember not to fill it to the top or it might burst. "We'll need your help," he told Smoky Woman.

"Anything."

He led her to the barricade and gave her Cain's rifle and pistol. "You stay with your brother. No matter what happens, don't let those savages get in here."

"You go alone?"

"One of us has to," Nate responded, and set down the Hawken. He wanted his hands free to carry the water bag and to bring his pistols into play when the savages tried to stop him, as they surely would. Giving her a reassuring smile while butterflies swarmed in his stomach, Nate placed a hand on top of the barricade and tensed to vault over it.

Chapter
Ten

Flying Hawk suddenly stepped forward and grasped Nate's arm, then he addressed his sister, speaking swiftly.

"What does he want?" Nate asked when the warrior finished.

"Want both you go," Smoky Woman translated.

"No. Tell him he must defend the cave. If we both went, and if we both should be taken captive or worse, you'd be on your own. I can't allow that," Nate said. He waited impatiently as his words were relayed. Then, before the warrior could lodge another objection, he vaulted over the barricade and instantly broke into a run, going at his top speed toward the spring. Once again he hugged the wall, but little good it did him.

Nate had not covered ten feet when a chorus of shrill whoops signified the savages had spotted him. A grimy brute popped up as if spewed from the earth itself and bore down on him with an uplifted club. Nate's right hand flashed for a pistol. The next moment a streaking shaft struck the savage on the side of the neck and went completely through, the bloody point protruding six inches. Staggered, the savage stumbled, clutched at the shaft, then whirled and made for another boulder.

Nate never broke stride. A lance glittered as it arced on high, swooped down at him, and thudded into the earth a yard to his rear. Darts rained down, a few at first, then more and more. He began weaving and ducking to make it harder for them to hit him. When he drew within 20 feet of the pool he nearly died.

A chunk of rock the size of his thigh came hurtling down from above, missing his by less than six inches, and slammed with terrific force into the ground. Unable to stop, he tripped over the rock and sprawled onto his hands and knees. Twisting, he shot a glance at the rim and saw several heads outlined against the sky just as one of the savages shoved a large boulder over the edge.

Nate flung himself away from the wall and rolled. He heard a tremendous crash, and swore the earth shook when the boulder smashed down on the exact spot where he had tripped. Pushing erect, he raced madly for the spring.

A dart nearly took off his nose.

Then he was there, dropping to his knees and shoving the open water bag under the surface. Bubbles rose in a flurry. One hand holding the bag, he shifted to check behind him.

Two savages, one armed with a lance, the other a club, were rapidly closing.

His pistol blossomed in his hand and spat smoke and lead. The savage with the lance, shot in the shoulder, jerked at the impact and fell. Fearlessly the second savage came on, his club waving in the air above his head.

Nate dared not let go of the water bag. It was becoming heavier and heavier as it filled, and if he let go it

123

might sink to the bottom. He was forced to tuck the spent flintlock under his belt and draw his other one with his left hand alone, which slowed him down so much that the savage was almost upon him before he got the other pistol out. The club whizzed at his head. Dropping low, Nate hastily pointed the pistol at the man and fired. He meant to send the ball into the savage's chest but in his haste he shot too low.

The ball bored into the Indian's groin, sheering off part of his organ. Howling like a banshee, the savage dropped his club and clutched his shattered manhood. He looked at Nate, his lips flecked with spittle, his eyes aflame with hatred.

Nate hit him, a short swipe of the flintlock that clipped the Indian on the temple and brought the man to his knees, stunned. As Nate raised the pistol for another blow the savage abruptly surged straight at him, head lowered, a human battering ram. Nate tried to get his arm down to block the rush but failed. In dismay he felt the man's head slam into his chest, propelling his rearward, into the pool.

A cool, wet blanket enveloped his body. He sank under to his chin. Somehow he retained his grip on the water bag and the pistol. His legs thrashing to keep him afloat, he saw the savage also in the pool, treading water and reaching for him with thick fingers formed into crushing claws.

Nate evaded the Indian's clutches, pedaling backwards. He had to get out of the pool and get out fast. Should another savage appear he'd be killed in an instant. Angling to the left, he swam for the edge, hauling the almost full water bag in his wake. The savage pursued him, swimming awkwardly, weakly, a crimson ring forming around the man's midsection and spreading upward.

Yet another dart splashed into the pool within a hand's width of Nate's face. Breathing heavily, he reached the rock rim, his right arm aching terribly from the weight of the bag. He hooked his left elbow on the rim, bunched his shoulder muscles, and pulled himself out.

What he needed most was a respite to catch his breath, but Fate dictated otherwise. A pair of iron hands clamped on his neck from behind and he was bodily lifted into the air. In order to fight back he had to release the water bag, which fell under his feet, water pouring from the narrow neck.

Nate lashed backwards with his right elbow and felt it connect with what seemed like a solid slab of marble. He tried the same tactic with his left elbow, slanting it higher, and this time connected with the savage's cheek. Simultaneously he kicked to the rear, driving his foot up and in, knowing his life hung in the balance.

Gurgling in rage, the savage heaved Nate aside as if he was no more than a child's doll. Nate landed hard on his right side, pain lancing from his elbow to his shoulder. His arm tingled, going numb as he stood. He still held a useless pistol in his left arm, which he wielded as a club when the savage sprang.

Although shorter, the savage was much heavier, so much so that Nate lost his balance and fell, the Indian on top of him. He found himself looking into the darkest, beadiest, most animal-like eyes he had ever seen on another human being, so bestial they reminded him of the eyes of bears. And in those eyes gleamed the promise of his death.

Desperately Nate slammed the flintlock onto the man's jaw, but the savage was unaffected. Those thick fingers closed on his throat, shutting off his windpipe. In less than a minute he would lose consciousness if his neck wasn't crushed before then. Gritting his teeth, he managed to move his tingling right arm and grab his tomahawk. The savage's thumbs were gouging deep into his throat and he thought his flesh would be pried apart.

Nate wrenched the tomahawk free, swung it out to the side, then drove the wide razor edge into the Indian's torso below the left arm. With a pantherish screech, the savage let go and leaped upright, a hand pressed to the profusely bleeding wound above his ribs.

Twisting, Nate pressed his advantage, arcing the tomahawk in a tight half-circle that brought the blade down on top of the savage's foot. The toes were chopped clean off and a red geyser spurted from the stub.

The savage, howling in fury, lifted his foot and clasped it. Behind him the Indian with the wounded groin was trying to climb out of the pool.

Nate's foot flicked out and crunched into the knee of the savage in front of him, knocking the man backwards into the Indian struggling to clamber from the water. Both men plunged under the surface. In the clear at last, Nate slid the pistol under his belt, scooped up the water bag in his left hand, and ran for the cave.

Darts zipped from several directions. Big stones were hurled down at him from above. A lance came close to bringing his down.

A whirlwind of motion, Nate constantly zigzagged, never running in a straight line for more than a few feet at a time. He saw Flying Hawk jump over the barricade and begin shooting arrows at an incredible rate, covering him. His foot hit a rut and he tripped, almost falling but righting himself with a supreme effort at the last moment.

Then he was near the cave and sailing because he'd successfully thwarted death and bucked the odds. He saw Smoky Woman behind the barricade, smiling too because now they had enough water to get by for a while, more than enough to use to keep Cain's fever under control. But their joy was premature and short-lived.

He dashed past Flying Hawk, and tensed to leap over the barricade when something jarred his left hand. Assuming he had banged the water bag against the barricade, he went on over and dropped to his knees to catch his breath. Caked with sweat, he wiped a sleeve across his brow, then stuck the tomahawk under his belt and turned to the water bag.

Smoky Woman's gasp echoed his own.

A dart had struck the bag at the bottom, rupturing the old skin and creating a hole several inches in diameter. The water was pouring out, and already over half of the contents had spilled onto the dry earth.

Frantically Nate scooped the bag up and tried to stem the flow with his hand, to no avail. Rising, he ran to the chamber, to the pot, and emptied what was left into it. Barely an inch covered the bottom of the pot when the last drop splashed down.

Disheartened, Nate looked at Solomon Cain, and was surprised to see him awake and alert although coated with perspiration from the fever. Cain glanced from the water bag to the pot to Nate's face.

"You made it to the spring, I take it."

Nate wearily nodded.

"Thank you for tryin'," Cain said, and coughed. "You share that water amongst yourselves. There's no need to waste any of it on me."

"Don't talk foolishness."

"I'm no fool, King. I'm burnin' up inside. My wound is infected. There's poison in my system."

"You'll pull through."

"Like hell. I ain't goin' to make it and you know it."

A low cry heralded Smoky Woman's rush to Cain's side. "Not talk this way! You strong! You live!"

"I'd surely like to," Cain met her gaze. "But bein' as strong as an ox don't count for much when the Reaper comes a-callin'. Even an ox dies sometimes."

Nate dropped the water bag and put a hand on Smoky Woman's shoulder. "Pay him no mind. It's the fever talking. We'll see to it that he gets out of here alive."

She knelt and touched Cain's face. "We need water. Much water."

"I'll try again as soon as I'm rested up," Nate proposed.

Cain tried to sit up but couldn't. "Now who's talkin' foolishness?" he rasped. "Those bastards out there ain't about to let you reach the pool a second time. They'll keep a real close guard on it, and they'll be ready for you if you try."

"I have no choice."

"Yes, you do. Come nightfall you have to get Smoky Woman out of here. Take that pigheaded brother of hers and light out for the mountains to the east. By mornin' you'll be in the clear."

"And what about you?"

Cain vented a bitter laugh. "I know my time has run its course. You just leave me here. I couldn't ride far anyway."

"We're not about to desert you," Nate declared, thinking that a day or so earlier he might have been differently inclined. "If we leave, you're leaving with us. And that's final."

"I'm surrounded by pigheads," Cain muttered.

Smoky Woman gently touched his lips and said sternly, "You be quiet! Rest until better."

Leaving them, Nate walked to the barricade and occupied himself with reloading both pistols while contemplating what to do. He had to admit that Cain was right. The savages would be clustered around the pool as thick as bees around a hive. He'd never make it there and back a second time. And since they couldn't very well stay in the cave and let themselves be starved into submission, they had to do just as Cain had proposed: cut out after dark.

They would ride light, taking only a parfleche or two filled with food. The rest of Cain's provisions—and the packs of gold—would have to be left behind.

He debated whether they should split up or stick together, and decided on the latter. There was strength in numbers, and if one of them went down the others would be right there to help. The next issue to decide was which direction to take. Going to the north was impossible because of the cliff, and riding westward, even though the land was flat and relatively open, would necessitate making too wide a loop through hostile territory in order to swing around and reach the mountain range to the east. If they went to the south they'd come on the dry wash, which he suspected harbored a few savages since it was an ideal spot to hide. So the only option left them was to ride like hell to the east, up and over the rise before the savages pierced then with lances and darts. Once they had the rise behind them, they could easily outdistance their pursuers.

Or so he hoped, anyway, as he finished reloading the flintlocks and wedged them under his belt. Retrieving the Hawken, he suddenly realized the Ute was staring pointedly at him. "You have a question?" he signed.

"I have an idea," the warrior clarified.

"Tell me."

Flying Hawk glanced at the bend, then moved closer to sign, "I say we give False Tongue to them. He is the one to blame for this, and he will not live long anyway. If we tie him to one of the horses and send the horse out, the strange ones who seek to count coup on us will go after him. While they are busy we can escape."

The cruel suggestion further impressed Nate with Flying Hawk's hatred of Cain. And while he could understand the Ute's feelings, he couldn't condone them. "Do you think your sister will stand by and do nothing while we send False Tongue to his death?"

"You can hold her while I do what is needed."

"No. I will not take sides in your dispute."

"Why do you care what happens to False Tongue? Look at all the trouble he had brought down on your head. You should want to see him dead as much as I do."

"I will not be a party to killing a man who can not defend himself."

Flying Hawk uttered an explosive "Wagh!" and turned away in disgust.

Nate didn't attempt to press the matter. He recognized doing so would be futile. Flying Hawk was too blinded by bigotry to ever listen to the moderating voice of reason, Only Cain's death would satisfy the Ute.

Nate went to the horses and gave Pegasus a rubdown. The gelding and the other two mounts stood with their heads hung low, hungry and thirsty and hot. Regrettably, there wasn't enough room for any of them to lie down. All three had relieved themselves in the passageway during the night and the smell was becoming worse by the hour.

Nate waited a sufficient length of time for Flying Hawk to cool down, then went over and broached the subject of leaving once night fell. The Ute made no comment until the very end.

"Who will Cain ride with? It will not be me."

"I have the fastest horse so I'll be the one," Nate volunteered, keenly aware of the disadvantage he would face when the time came for them to flee. He saw Flying Hawk smile. Why? Was the warrior inwardly gloating because he knew it would be a miracle if Nate and Cain got further than 30 yards from the cave?

Brooding, he sat down near the barricade and spent the next several hours racking his brain for another way out of their fix. He considered everything from sneaking out and trying to pick the savages off one by one to starting a huge fire at the cave entrance and escaping under cover of the smoke. Few of his ideas were practical. None were appealing. If they sneaked out the savages would probably pick them off instead. And thick smoke would blind them as well as the Indians, slowing them down during the precious span of seconds when they'd need all the speed their mounts could muster.

The golden sun climbed steadily upward, passed its zenith, and slid toward the western horizon. Outside nothing moved. The landscape gave off shimmering waves of heat that distorted objects in the distance.

Nate used an old trick that made a person salivate more than usual to partially ease his thirst; he stuck a pebble in his mouth. About two in the afternoon Flying Hawk asked him to stand watch for a while alone, and he agreed. The warrior promptly went back to the chamber. Shortly thereafter angry voices could be heard.

As Nate surveyed the ground outside he saw that the bodies of the Indians slain that morning had all vanished. Like the Apaches, these savages never left their dead behind, perhaps out of fear the bodies would be mutilated. Of course, they hadn't been able to get the ones in the cave. Yet.

The heat and the lack of activity combined to produce waves of drowsiness, which he fought off with repeated shakes of his head. To pass the time and to stay awake he sharpened his butcher knife and the tomahawk.

A while later Flying Hawk returned. His lips were thin slits, his eyes blazing with fury. "She will not listen to me!" he signed angrily.

Nate responded with, "If there is one important lesson I have learned from being married, it is that women have minds of their own. They do not like for men to tell them what to do. Most do not even like for men to make suggestions. So your sister is no exception. Women are more independent than most men give them credit for being."

"I am only concerned for her," Flying Hawk signed. "I do not want to see her spend the rest of her life in misery." He paused. "She belongs with my people, not with yours."

"She belongs wherever she will be happiest, and you have made it plain that your people will not take kindly to her having a child fathered by a white man."

"I have influence in our councils. I might be able to persuade our people to accept the child."

"And if you failed?"

"The Utes are many, with many villages. We would find one where they would allow my sister to live in peace, where they would let her child live as a Ute should."

Here was an unexpected development. Previously Flying Hawk had been unwilling to countenance the child's birth; now the warrior was willing to help his sister raise the child if she would stay with their people. There was hope for the man after all, Nate reflected wryly. "Smoky Woman does not want to do this?" he asked.

"No," Flying Hawk gestured sharply. "She still wants to live with False Tongue among your kind. All my words were wasted on her ears." He looked at Nate. "Would you talk to her?"

"It is not my place."

"Or is it that you do not agree with me? Do you believe she would be better off among your people than mine?"

"What I think does not count. She has made her decision and nothing I could say would change it."

Scowling, Flying Hawk leaned both arms on the top of the barricade, effectively ending their conversation.

The remainder of the afternoon passed in strained silence. Nate kept to himself and the warrior did the same. When, eventually, the shadows lengthened and the sun neared the horizon, Nate stirred and signed, "It is time to get ready."

He saddled Pegasus and brought the Palouse close to the barricade, then let the reins dangle. His parfleches were easy to locate and he strapped them on behind the saddle. The other horses were left bareback for the Utes.

Smoky Woman had Cain's head cradled on her lap and was wiping his face with a damp cloth when Nate entered. Mercifully Cain had passed out again.

"We'll be leaving soon," he announced.

"Him very weak."

"I know. We'll use some rope and tie him to me so he won't fall off."

"Tie him to me."

Nate touched her elbow. "I'm a mite bigger and stronger than you are. He's less likely to pull me off if he starts to fall."

Lambent pools of abiding affection were turned on him. "He pressed to my heart."

"I know."

"Take care of him."

"I will," Nate pledged sincerely.

Flying Hawk lent a reluctant hand at Nate's request in carrying the unconscious man from the chamber. They moved slowly to avoid jostling Cain, who mumbled the whole time, and set him down on his back next to Pegasus. Nate swung up, then inched forward as far as he could to make room for Cain.

While Smoky Woman helped to hold Solomon steady, Flying Hawk brought the rope over. With Nate helping, they quickly looped it several times around Cain's lower back and Nate's midsection, arranging the knot so it was just above Nate's buckle where he could get at it readily.

Smoky Woman mounted, Cain's pistol in her right hand, his rifle in her left, her eyes locked on the man she loved.

The warrior, ducking low, went to the end of the barricade and rolled the corpses aside to make an opening for the horses. Scooting back, he held his bow in his right hand and climbed onto the third animal.

Nate could feel the heavy weight of Cain's body pressing against him, compelling him to stiffen his back muscles to stay upright. It wasn't that Cain was heavy. Quite the contrary. But in Cain's current state he was just so much dead weight. Suddenly Nate was taken aback to feel Cain stir feebly.

"What the hell is goin' on? Why am I on a horse?"

"We're cutting out, Solomon," Nate said, twisting his head. "So shush until we're in the clear."

Cain blinked a few times, his forehead furrowed. "The gold, King? Are you bringing the gold?"

There was a despondent, pleading quality to Cain's tone that caused Nate to do something he rarely did. "Yes, we're taking it with us. Now don't talk and hold on tight."

A weak nod was Cain's reply.

Outside, twilight had claimed the wasteland. Nate held the reins loosely in his right hand, the Hawken tight in his left, and anxiously waited for the darkness to deepen. Solomon Cain passed out again and began breathing deeply. Pegasus fidgeted. So did the other horses. All three were eager to leave the cramped confines of the cave.

At last Nate judged the time to be ripe, and with a lash of the reins and a poke of his heels he rode Pegasus out into the ominous night.

Chapter
Eleven

The moment Nate was clear of the cave he reined to the left and galloped toward the rise, Smoky Woman and Flying Hawk right behind him. Twelve hoofs drummed in staccato rhythm, clattering on the rocky ground, making enough racket to alert every savage within a quarter of a mile. A harsh cry to the south was attended by a series of cries from the vicinity of the spring and a couple more from on top of the cliff.

Pegasus was a pied-colored streak, his head level with his flowing body, his mane flying. It was all Nate could do to stay in the saddle. Not because of the gelding. Solomon Cain was flapping wildly against him and swaying with every stride the Palouse took, threatening to topple them both. Too late Nate discovered the rope wasn't holding Cain as securely as he'd thought it would.

On he galloped anyway, knowing to slow down now was certain suicide. The rise loomed directly ahead. He swept up the slope, and had gotten a third of the way to the top when to his rear a horse whinnied in pain and there was a tremendous crash.

Now Nate did slow and glance back. He was horrified to see Smoky Woman's mount had gone down, a lance jutting from its heaving side. She had lost both guns in the tumble but was unhurt. Springing up, she lifted her arms at a yell from her brother. The next second Flying Hawk reached her and yanked her roughly up behind him. Then, using his bow as a quirt, the warrior started up the slope.

Darts were flying fast and thick. Lances cleaved the air. The enraged cries of the pursuing savages would have brought gooseflesh to a dead man.

Nate goaded Pegasus upward. The gelding had lost a lot of momentum and struggled to go faster. A whizzing dart clipped Nate's shoulder but didn't draw any blood. Another nicked the Palouse's ear and did.

"Go! Go!" Nate urged, slapping his legs against Pegasus's sides. All it would take was one lucky hit and any hope of escape would be shattered. He heard Cain groan and imagined the pain the man must be feeling, but there was nothing he could do about it until they were far, far away.

Suddenly Smoky Woman yelled something in Ute.

Looking back, Nate saw Flying Hawk hunched low over their mount and Smoky Woman tugging furiously at her brother's shoulder. He understood why when her hand appeared clutching a bloody dart. The warrior, his teeth clenched, straightened and kept on coming.

Just a little further! Nate told himself. Just a little further and they would be over the crest and safe from the deluge of darts and spears. Only 20 feet to go. Then 15. Then ten. He whooped for joy when Pegasus plunged down the other side, then caught himself and looked back at the Utes.

Brother and sister were hard on his heels.

Nate smiled broadly. They'd done it! A tingle of excitement at their deliverance coursed through him, only to be tempered by the sight of dark shapes appearing at the top of the rise. The savages were still after them and coming on fast!

Bending forward, Nate rode for his life and the life of the man strapped to his back. More darts reined down. Flying Hawk's horse neighed wildly but continued to race pell-mell across the sinister wasteland.

Soon the darts stopped seeking them. The shapes of the savages evaporated in the gloom.

Nate was exceptionally alert to the flow of the terrain. A misstep now could cost Pegasus or the other horse a broken leg. So he studied the land ahead with care. Thanks to a sliver of moon he could see well enough to avoid obstacles such as ruts, boulders, and crevices.

For 20 minutes they rode hard, until Nate was positive they were safe. Then he reined up in a spray of dust and waited for the Utes to catch up. During the flight they had fallen a dozen yards behind, and now, as they drew to a stop alongside him, their horse wheezed and stumbled.

Smoky Woman was off the animal in a lithe bound. Her brother, wincing, dismounted slowly and stood with a hand pressed to his wounded shoulder.

Nate was staring aghast at the horse. The poor animal had taken three darts, one in the neck and two in the side. Dark stains caused by copiously flowing blood marked its coat. Additional blood trickled from its flaring nostrils.

"How Cain?" Smoky Woman asked, stepping up and resting a hand on Solomon's thigh.

"Doing fine, near as I can tell," Nate said. He tugged at the stubborn knot, then impatiently whipped out his butcher knife and sliced the loops in half.

Cain promptly sagged, his chin touching his chest, and started to fall off. Instantly Smoky Woman braced him with her hands and said, "Help, please!"

Quickly sliding off, Nate jammed the knife into its sheath and took hold of Cain's waist to ease him from the saddle. Smoky Woman grasped Cain's slack legs. Together they carefully lowered him to the ground, onto his back, and she knelt to examine him closely, running her hands over his body as she probed for darts.

The wounded horse picked that moment to take a few steps, halt, and nicker pathetically. Staggering, it tottered to the left. Then its front knees buckled and it sank down, puffing like a steam engine.

Closer scrutiny showed Nate that the dart in the animal's neck was so firmly imbedded as to be impossible to get out by hand. It would have to be dug out with a knife. The other two, though, protruded enough to be firmly grasped, so with vigorous pulling he was able to pluck them loose. The horse whinnied in agony as the second was extracted, and a torrent of fresh blood pumped from the hole.

Nate cast the darts from him with an angry jerk. If they had the time and enough water and forage they might be able to nurse the wounded animal back to health. But of course they had none of those things. The poor horse was doomed and there was nothing he could do except put it out of its misery now rather than let it linger on for a few days in the most abominable torment. And he couldn't use a gun since the sound of a shot would carry for a mile or more in the rarified mountain air.

The hilt of the butcher knife molded to his palm as he stepped up to the horse's neck and felt for the telltale jugular groove. Draping his left arm over the neck, he squeezed to keep the neck still long enough for his right hand to slash open the jugular, then he jumped back before the crimson geyser that spurted forth could drench him.

Again the horse nickered, soft and low, and shook its head as if at buzzing flies. Its great breaths became more labored than ever. Slowly the head drooped.

Nate turned, unwilling to watch the animal die. He disliked having to dispatch it. His only consolation was that according to some old-timers he had talked to, bleeding to death was a painless way to go. There was little if any pain. It was more like the sensation of falling asleep, all drowsy and tingly and bizarrely pleasant.

Smoky Woman had her hand on Cain's forehead. "Him still much hot," she said.

"He'll be all right once we're in the mountains," Nate said, although inwardly he lacked complete conviction. First they must get Cain there, which promised to be a formidable task given there might be more savages around. And too, infections were difficult to eliminate under the best of circumstances; they still had many miles to travel across the inhospitable pocket of desolation, which would only make Cain's condition worse.

Nate glanced at Flying Hawk, who stood stoically nearby. "How are you?" he signed, as usual amplifying his motions so they would be easily understood in the dark.

The warrior grunted.

"Let me see," Nate signed, moving behind him. The dart, he saw, had penetrated several inches and left a finger-sized hole when it had been wrenched out. Thankfully, the wound had stopped bleeding, indicating the dart had not severed any large blood vessels.

Solomon Cain groaned and tossed as would someone having a bad dream.

"We have to press on," Nate said.

"Cain need rest," Smoky Woman objected.

"When we're safe. We haven't gone all that far yet, and for all we know our enemies can run long distances without tiring, just like the Apaches do. They might be closing in on us even as we speak. When we reach the mountains he can rest."

She thought for a moment, then rose and pointed at the gelding. "You go ahead. Take Cain."

Now it was Nate's turn to object. "I'm not leaving Flying Hawk and you here all alone," he declared.

"You go fast," she insisted. "We come later."

Should he or shouldn't he? Nate wondered. She had a valid point, namely that he could get Cain to safety, to that sheltered park where the grass was green and the water deliciously cold, well before dawn if he rode off right that minute. There Cain would get all the rest he needed. But Nate balked at the idea of deserting the two Utes, leaving them stranded, afoot, with Flying Hawk hurt. They would be unable to stand off the savages if they were found. Sighing, he said, "No. We'll stay together."

Simmering with frustration, Smoky Woman clenched her fists. "You go fast. Get Cain safe."

"No. We go together," Nate emphasized as he stooped and slid both hands under Cain's shoulders. A look and a nod at Flying Hawk was sufficient to bring the warrior over, and presently they had Cain in the saddle with his legs tied tight to the stirrups and additional rope securing him to the saddle horn.

Nate grasped the reins and assumed the lead, but he only took a single pace when the reins were torn from his grasp by Smoky Woman, who angrily motioned for him to keep walking. She intended to take care of Cain herself.

"As you wish," Nate said softly, going on. Her resentment upset him, yet not enough to make him change his mind. There were four lives at stake, not just one, and he had a responsibility to do his damnedest to insure all four of them survived. She would thank him, later, if they ran into trouble.

The minutes dragged past as if weighted with an anchor. A total and unnatural quiet pervaded their surroundings. Missing were the typical night sounds of yipping coyotes, howling wolves, hooting owls, and snarling panthers. Even the insects, if there were any, were silent.

Nate checked to their rear time and again. His warning about the savages being able to duplicate the feats of the Apaches was no idle chatter. Apaches were marvelous long-distance runners, able to cover 70 miles at a steady dogtrot. It was very possible the Diggers or Root Eaters, if such they were, could do the same.

Occasionally he tilted his head back to admire the magnificent celestial display overhead. Back in New York City, he had barely looked at the stars. Out here, among the mile-high Rockies, they resembled brilliant torches, flaring bright and proud in the sprawling firmament, countless in number, awesome in aspect. He never tired of viewing the nightly spectacle.

A faint scratching noise wafted on the breeze.

Pausing, Nate gazed to the northwest but saw nothing to arouse concern. Whether man or beast or freak of Nature had made the sound, he had no way of determining. Shrugging, he hiked on, staring at the inky silhouettes of the eastern range which seemed so very far away.

Flying Hawk joined his sister and the two conversed in soft whispers. The warrior, Nate noticed, held his right arm bent close to his body, evidence the shoulder wound was bothering him severely.

By Nate's reckoning an hour and a half had elapsed when they came to a ridge of caprock. At its base Smoky

Woman halted and cast a critical eye at him. "We stop little bit?" she asked.

Nate didn't see any harm in a few minutes of rest. "Yes."

With her brother's aid, Smoky Woman took Cain down and laid him on a flat stretch of solid rock. She borrowed her brother's knife to cut a strip from the hem of her buckskin dress, then moistened the strip with her spittle so she could cool Cain's face and neck.

Nate thought to open a parfleche and remove several pieces of jerked venison. He offered one to Flying Hawk, who accepted it with a nod, and to Smoky Woman, who vigorously shook her head. He extended his hand, saying, "You really should eat something. You need to keep up your strength." But to his consternation, she swatted his hand aside and shifted so her back was to him.

Deeply chagrined, Nate moved a couple of yards off and sat with his left shoulder propped against a boulder. So that was the thanks he got for trying to do the right thing! She didn't want to have anything to do with him.

He chewed absently, barely aware of the tangy taste that normally he liked so much. Gazing around, he realized Flying Hawk was staring at him. When he ventured a friendly smile, the Ute turned away. Puzzled, he scratched his chin and tried to make sense of the warrior's behavior. Were they both mad at him? Smoky Woman he could understand, but not her brother.

A few minutes later Nate stood and coughed to clear his throat. "We should be moving on," he proposed.

Without saying a word, Smoky Woman and Flying Hawk put Cain back on Pegasus. They tied him as before. Then Smoky Woman took the reins and moved out, staying close to the base of the ridge. Her brother fell into step behind her, leaving Nate to follow at his leisure.

Slanting the Hawken over his left shoulder, Nate did just that. He was almost sorry he hadn't taken Smoky Woman up on her request to ride off with Cain. It would serve them right, he reflected, if the savages caught up with them when he wasn't on hand to help in the fight.

Shortly thereafter Nate dimly heard an indistinct noise, this time to the south. Peering into the darkness proved unavailing. If there was something or someone out there, they were virtual ghosts.

He kept a close watch on their back trail from then on. If the savages were dogging them, the attack, when it came, would be swift and silent. He imagined getting a dart between the shoulder blades, and his skin prickled from head to toe.

Presently the wind picked up, gusting violently as it often did in the high country. There were no trees to rustle, no grass to bend, but it did howl among the benches and gorges, the bluffs and the canyons, moaning and wailing like a forlorn soul fated to endlessly wander the earth in search of eternal rest.

Nate hoped a storm wasn't approaching. Solomon Cain couldn't withstand a steady soaking; weakened as he was, Cain would come down with the chills, perhaps even contract pneumonia. Scanning the heavens confirmed the sky was cloudless, alleviating Nate's fears.

The encounter with the primitive Indians gave Nate cause to wonder how many other unknown tribes existed west of the Mississippi. The vast territory was essentially unexplored, so who could say what lurked in the depths of the verdant forests or in remote recesses like the wasteland he was now in? He'd heard tales of Indians living in fabulous cliff cities far to the southwest, and fantastic stories of Indians living on the northern Pacific Coast who hunted huge whales from flimsy craft. Previously he had been skeptical of any and all such reports, but the more he learned of the limitless land of mystery in which he had elected to dwell, the more he appreciated the truth of the age-old belief that there were more things in heaven and on earth than humankind dreamed of. And some of them were better left alone.

One day, though, Nate wanted to venture to the Pacific Ocean and perhaps explore regions of the continent seldom if ever visited by white men. Abiding within him was a perpetual curiosity about what might lie beyond the next horizon. He'd like to see those cliff cities and watch a boatload of Indians hunt one of the great whales. He'd like to penetrate to the heart of the many wonders waiting to be discovered by those bold enough to challenge the unknown.

When that day would come, he had no idea. For now he had a wife and son to think of. Providing for them was his first priority. He felt confident that at some point in the future an opportunity would arise to satisfy his craving to explore. Until then he would be patient.

His short sleep of the night before had done little to refresh him, and now the toll of the long day and the desperate flight brought fatigue to his limbs and drowsiness to his mind. Often his heavy eyelids tried to stay shut, and he would energetically shake his head and yawn each time as he fought to stay alert.

Solomon Cain commenced snoring, a low rumble like that of a hibernating bear.

Nate wished the man would stop. The snoring would drown out any slight noises that might herald an attack by the savages. He forced his sluggish faculties to razor sharpness and scoured the empty landscape on all sides. Not a hint of movement could be detected.

Then he got a surprise. He saw Smoky Woman hand the reins to her brother and come back to fall into step beside him.

"I sorry," she said softly in her heavily accented English.

"For what?" Nate responded without thinking.

"For treating you poorly."

"You had your reasons, I reckon."

"No excuse. You do what right by stay with us. Brother make that clear."

"He did?" Nate replied in mild amazement that the Ute had spoken up in his defense. "I figured he was mad at me too."

"Him not like whites, but him say you man of honor."

"Be sure and thank your brother for the compliment."

They strolled for a score of yards in taciturn introspection. Then Smoky Woman fixed her beautiful eyes on him.

"I love Cain."

"I know."

"You must understand. I never love man before, not like this. When Cain take me I much scared. But him nice. Him gentle. I think him pretty."

Nate listened attentively, mystified as to why she was baring her soul. She owed him no explanations. It was none of his business. Yet she went on talking, struggling to find the proper words, pausing between sentences to formulate her thoughts.

"Cain not like any man. He fire my heart, make me forget my people, my family. All I want was him."

True love, Nate mused, did have a way of jangling a person's brain so badly they couldn't think straight. Sweet memories of his first meeting with Winona reminded him of how he had been utterly swept away by her looks, her touch, even her scent. The mere sight of her had been enough to set his pulse to racing.

"Cain must not die. Our child have him for father."

Was it Nate's imagination, or did he read a certain tinge of anxiety in her tone? He could sympathize with her plight. If she lost Cain, she'd be on her own, raising a half-breed son or daughter in a world hostile to breeds, a taxing task that would make her old before her time.

Smoky Woman placed a hand on her stomach and smiled. "We be happy always. Child have much love. Grow to be good."

"Your child will be very fortunate," Nate declared. "Believe me, I want things to work out for you as much as you do yourself. And if you still want me to, I'll ride on ahead to the mountains with Cain once we're close enough and I'm convinced the other tribe isn't after us."

She impulsively gave his elbow a friendly squeeze. "Thank you, Grizzly Killer."

There was an odd lump in Nate's throat as he watched her return to her brother and take over leading the Palouse. Her love was so sincere, so pure. But what about Cain's love for her? Did Cain truly care for her, or had he pretended to care because he craved her companionship? If Nate was any judge, the only thing Solomon Cain cared about was the gold.

At last the lonesome wail of a distant wolf wavered on the crisp air.

Nate perked up and scanned the eastern range. They must be within a mile or so of the mountains! Then he had second thoughts. They'd not gone far enough yet. The wolf must be prowling the eastern perimeter of the wasteland and was trying to locate others of its kind.

Suddenly Smoky Woman and Flying Hawk halted. Pegasus whinnied and shied away, as if from a snake in his path.

In four bounds Nate learned the reason. They had unexpectedly come on a sheer drop-off of 50 or 60 feet, a slope impossible for the gelding to negotiate. "We'll have to go around," he advised, moving to the left along the rim.

The bottom was lost in the bleak gloom. It might well be a sepulchral pit, but he wouldn't know until he found

146

a way down. He was encouraged by the fact the rim angled gradually lower.

A blast of wind struck him, flapping the whangs on his buckskins. It brought with it the weird cry of an unknown bird, the same bird he'd heard when he'd been after Smoky Woman's abductors. Only it wasn't a bird.

Stopping, Nate raised the Hawken and sought the source of the cry. A squat, pale form briefly materialized over a hundred feet off, then seemed to dissipate on the blustering breeze. Nate's stomach bound into knots as he hurried on, motioning for the others to do the same. Isolated on the rim as they were, with their backs to the drop-off, they were particularly vulnerable. They had to reach flat ground or find a spot to take shelter.

But the savages weren't about to let them. There was a sharp shout in an unfamiliar tongue, and a half-dozen shapes rose up and charged.

Chapter
Twelve

Nate took speedy aim and fired, rushing his shot so much he was certain he missed. The intended target, and all the rest of the savages, promptly went to ground. "Keep going!" he urged the Utes, letting them take the lead so he could protect their flank and safeguard Pegasus.

A blurred object arced down from the inkwell sky, narrowly missing the gelding's neck and sailing out over the drop-off.

Drawing his right pistol, Nate searched in vain for an enemy to shoot. He berated himself for having stopped to rest earlier. Had they gone at a swifter pace, the primitives might not have overtaken them.

But such thoughts, he realized, were pointless. Survival was the issue. With that uppermost in mind, he took a gamble and wedged the pistol under his belt again so he could reload the rifle. Some of the powder spilled and he had a trying time inserting the ball and patch, yet when they came to the end of the incline the Hawken was loaded and cocked.

Smoky Woman cut eastward, walking faster. Flying Hawk stayed close to her, a shaft set to take wing.

Nate walked backward, his gaze roving over the rim they had just vacated. When several shifting forms appeared, he whipped the Hawken to his shoulder. Hesitation seized him. He'd already wasted one shot. Why waste another? Let the savages come nearer. Then he would show them why he had won a prime buffalo robe for his marksmanship at the Rendezvous the year before.

Huge boulders abruptly reared to the right and the left. On the one hand Nate was grateful for the cover. On the other he worried that the savages would take advantage of the situation by sneaking so close they couldn't miss. Logic told him the Indians would try to slay Pegasus first since killing the horse meant stranding their quarry.

The next moment Flying Hawk elevated his bow and let fly.

A short shriek testified to his accuracy.

Several darts served as retaliation. One smacked into the earth next to Smoky Woman. A second passed through the Palouse's swishing tail. The third flashed overhead.

A bold strategy occurred to Nate, and with a gesture at the warrior to go on, he darted behind a boulder they were passing and crouched with his back against the hard stone surface. The Utes and the gelding were soon dim figures in the night. Suddenly he heard the whispering tread of a stealthy stalker, and a heartbeat later a stout Indian stepped into view, a spear clutched in the man's brawny right hand. The Indian didn't see Nate, so intent was he on those he hunted.

Then the man halted, apparently aware one of the figures was missing.

Like a striking rattler, Nate pounced. Only he didn't use a gun. At the last instant he pulled his butcher knife and buried the keen blade in the savage's thick throat. The savage sprang rearward, his throat gushing red, and threw back his arm to hurl the spear. Belatedly, the shock of his wound staggered him and he shuffled weakly to the left, his spear arm waving.

Nate knew a dead man when he saw one. Whirling, he sprinted after his companions, sliding the damp knife into his sheath along the way. A harrowing reminder not to make rash judgments jolted him when the spear whizzed over his left shoulder. Twisting, he saw the savage collapse.

Increasing his speed, he soon came on Flying Hawk and Smoky Woman. The warrior had trained an arrow on him. Then those eagle eyes recognized who he was and the bow lowered fractionally. Side by side they followed Pegasus, covering a hundred yards before they were made aware of their blunder. One of them should have been in front of the gelding.

It was Smoky Woman's scream that caused them both to spin, and they both saw the muscular savage bearing down on her with a club held aloft. Nate sighted, but as quick as he was he wasn't quick enough, because Flying Hawk got off a shaft first, the arrow flying straight and true, the barbed point biting into the savage's chest above the heart.

Like a poled ox the savage toppled.

Flying Hawk dashed forward, leaving Nate to protect their rear alone. He anticipated another onslaught of darts and spears, but none was forthcoming. Every nerve vibrant, he glued his thumb to the hammer, his finger to the trigger. One of the Indians was bound to appear sooner or later and he would be ready.

Bewilderingly, time went by and no more savages appeared. Nate couldn't believe the band had given up so easily. They must be lurking out there somewhere, he figured, waiting their chance. So he didn't relax for an instant. But after a while his body grew tired of its own accord. There was just so much strenuous exertion and nervous excitement a human being could handle, and he had been through sheer hell ever since finding Cain strung up from that tree.

The seconds turned into minutes, the minutes, inexplicably, into an hour, then two hours, and three.

During all this time Nate's vigilance inevitably waned, his weariness waxed. Despite the danger, he longed to lie down and sleep. The lack of hostile action lulled him into suspecting he was wrong; the savages had decided to take their dead and leave. Or so logical reasoning led him to believe. His gut instincts were another story.

A graying of the eastern sky promised the imminent arrival of dawn.

The mountains were close but not close enough, two miles or better if Nate was any judge of distance, two more miles of arid desolation frequented by a bloodthirsty band of feral savages. If, he vowed, he made it out, he'd never, ever return unless it was at the head of an army.

A high gorge bisected by a dry wash blocked their route. On either hand skeletal ridges resembled imposing medieval ramparts. They could go around or they could go on through. Flying Hawk chose the shorter path.

Dwarfed into insignificance by the size of the gorge, Nate tried not to dwell on what would happen if the savages gained the high ground and proceeded to dislodge some of the gigantic boulders balanced precariously up above. A single rock slide would crush all four of them and Pegasus to boot.

Nerves taunt, Nate trudged on, his gaze never leaving the tops of the walls. Here at the bottom of the gorge the feeble rays of approaching daylight had not yet reached, and it was as if they were walking through a night-shrouded realm. He could see Flying Hawk, but not the Ute's features when the warrior turned his head from side to side.

Was it half an hour that went by? Forty-five minutes? Estimating time was difficult when there was no point of reference such as the sun or the positions of the stars to judge by, and the few stars visible from the depths of the gorge were too indistinct to be of any aid.

Shortly thereafter, when the end of the gorge showed as a pale patch of light blue up ahead, the unforeseen transpired. Solomon Cain abruptly awakened and tried to sit up in the saddle.

"What the hell!" he blurted out loudly, his words echoing off the walls. "Why am I tied down?"

In a flash Nate was there and touching a hand to Cain's cheek. "Quiet or we're all dead!"

"King?" Cain said, twisting his head with an effort. He blinked, then coughed. "What the devil is going on? Where are we? Everything is all fuzzy in my noggin."

"We're trying to reach the mountains but those savages are after us. I don't think they know where we are, but they will if we're not mighty careful."

"Sorry," Cain muttered, and grasped the rope securing him to the saddle horn. "Was this necessary?"

"It was if we wanted to get you out in one piece. Otherwise you would have fallen off hours ago and busted your head open," Nate said. "We sure as blazes couldn't tote you out on our backs."

"Well, cut me loose. I think my fever has broke and I feel a heap better now. I can walk."

"Stay up there a while longer," Nate suggested, afraid Cain would slow them down on foot. Every moment counted, and he felt a compelling urgency to reach the range quickly.

"No, damn it!" Cain snapped. "I'm sore as hell and my back is all cramped up. So cut me free, damn you! I want to stretch my legs a spell."

Disinclined to comply, Nate shook his head, and was about to explain why when Smoky Woman touched his arm.

"Please, Grizzly Killer."

Against Nate's better judgment, he gave in. He justified doing so by reasoning that he had no right to keep Cain trussed up if the man didn't care to be. And he certainly didn't want to become embroiled in a shouting match that might attract the savages.

"I'm waitin'!" Cain barked.

"All right," Nate growled, drawing his knife. "But if you can't keep up, back on Pegasus you go." Short strokes parted the rope strands, and Solomon Cain, with a grateful sigh, slid off the Palouse into Smoky Woman's waiting arms.

"We must hurry," Nate prompted.

"Hold your horses," Cain shot back, embracing Smoky Woman so tightly she could barely move. "And quit your worryin' about those naked bastards. They're no account anyways you lays your sight."

Strange words coming from a man those "no account" savages had almost killed, Nate reflected, but he held his tongue. He also thought it odd when Cain gave Smoky Woman a passionate kiss right there in front of him. For all their bluster and bravado, mountain men were uncommonly shy about sexual matters and preferred to do their romancing in the privacy of their lodges or cabins. Public displays of intense affection were rare.

At length Cain broke the kiss, clasped Smoky Woman's dainty hand in his, and walked slowly toward the end of the gorge. Neither of them bothered about the Palouse.

Nate grabbed the reins and fell into step behind them. Flying Hawk brought up the rear.

"You know, King," Cain said softly over his shoulder, "I reckon my partner and me never ought to have come here. This place is cursed through and through. Any fool could of seen that. But not us. We wanted that gold and . . ." He stopped, glanced at the gelding, then glared at Nate. "Damn you! You told me you were bringin' the gold!"

"Keep your voice down," Nate urged.

"Like hell I will," Cain barked, letting go of Smoky Woman, his face livid. "Simon and I worked like slaves to dig that yellow ore out and you went and left it all behind! How could you?"

"It was either you or the gold. My horse couldn't carry both."

"You could have brought *some*!" Cain virtually wailed. "This coon didn't go to all that trouble to leave empty-handed! I'm goin' back." So saying, he started to brush past Nate.

"No!" Smoky Woman exclaimed.

Nate gripped Cain's wrist and held on. "Now it's your turn to hold your horses. You're in no condition to travel all the way back to the cave, and even if you were you'd have the savages dogging you every step of the way. Be sensible, Solomon. Stay with us."

Cain tried to tear his arm loose. "I'm a free man and I can do as I damn well please without your say-so. That gold is rightfully mine and I don't intend to leave it there for any old hoss to discover and steal. So let go."

"Not until you give me your word you'll give up the notion of going back."

"Never," Cain said, again striving to free his wrist. Suddenly, without any forewarning, he blanched and buckled, sagging forward.

Fortunately Nate was right there to catch him and lower him to the ground. "You blamed fool," Nate said. "See my point? You're in no shape to go anywhere."

A fit of coughing prevented Cain from answering. Eyes closed, fist pressed to his lips, he hacked uncontrollably. Smoky Woman came and knelt beside him to affectionately stroke his brow.

Rising, Nate stepped back and draped an arm on Pegasus. In all his travels he had seldom met anyone as contrary as the jackass on the ground. Cain never seemed to learn. Anyone else, anyone with a shred of common sense, would know Nate had done the right thing and let it go at that. But not Solomon. Cain's lust for gold was a sickness which not even love could cure.

Impatient to be off, Nate tapped his fingers on the saddle horn and touched a sticky substance. Closer inspection revealed a few large drops of drying blood, not on the saddle horn itself but on the leather strap to his possibles bag which he often draped over the horn when riding, a habit his mentor, Shakespeare McNair, had been trying to break him of ever since they met. "Always keep your possibles on your person," Shakespeare had often said. "You never know when you'll be left afoot."

Most trappers crammed their possibles bag with their tobacco and pipe, thread and needle, flints and steel, maybe their bait box for beaver, and other odds and ends. But because Nate didn't smoke tobacco and carried his flint and steel in his ammo pouch, he felt no need to tote the extra weight along except when out working a trap line.

Solomon was sitting up now, his head bowed low, breathing deep. "I reckon I'm nowhere near fit yet," he said, rasping out the words. "You're right, King. Much as I hate the idea, my gold will have to stay where it is until I can come back for it. Just don't get any notions about taking it for yourself. I'd hunt you down to the ends of the earth if need be."

"Don't threaten me," Nate said. "Don't *ever* threaten me."

The edge to Nate's voice made Cain stiffen. "I didn't mean to get you riled," he mumbled, gingerly touching his shoulder.

Nate noticed a dark stain. "Are you bleeding again'?"

"Could be. My shoulder does feel a mite damp now and then."

Nate scanned the top of the gorge. For a minute there he had forgotten all about the savages, an oversight he dared not repeat if he valued his life. "We must keep going. I'll check the bandage later. Can you walk or would you rather ride?"

"Never let it be said that a little thing like a busted shoulder turned me puny," Cain responded. "I'll walk, with your permission, your highness."

"Suit yourself." Nate assumed the lead once again, the gelding at his elbow. Pink and orange harbingers of dawn painted the eastern sky in broad strokes, and a slender sliver of gold rimmed the skyline. The increasing light even penetrated to the bottom of the gorge. Of the well-nigh limitless number of stars visible an hour ago, now only several shone bright enough to stand out, and soon they would fade too.

Near the gorge mouth Nate slowed. Jumbled boulders on either hand afforded an ideal ambush spot. If somehow the savages had gotten ahead of them, a distinct possibility given the delay caused by Cain, here was where the Indians would strike.

He cocked the Hawken and treaded on silent soles, a useless precaution since there was no way of muffling Pegasus's hoofs. Or was there? He could cut his blanket into four pieces and wrap one piece around each hoof. Why hadn't he thought of it sooner? Sometimes he acted as if he had buffalo chips for brains!

By now he was too near the boulders to stop for any reason. Should savages be lurking there, they'd speedily drop him with their spears or darts. Hawken leveled, he padded toward a golden bowl of sunlight past the boulders.

His apprehension proved unfounded. Not only were there no savages in hiding at the gorge, but before him unfolded a flat tract of arid terrain that stretched clear to the base of the eastern mountains, a tract where they would be perfectly safe because no one could get anywhere near them without being seen. Should a lizard move out there, he'd know it. No matter which direction the savages came from, his rifle and the Ute's bow would keep them at bay.

Nate chuckled to himself and forged on. A stroke of good luck at last! he reflected. In two hours they'd be among the dense pines covering the lower slopes of the mountains. They'd be safe. He planned to make camp at the spring in the park and stay there for four or five days, long enough for Cain to recover sufficiently to be able to continue eastward. Perhaps he could persuade Flying Hawk to bring them some horses from the Ute village. If not, well, he'd stick with Smoky Woman and Cain until they were in safer territory.

He inhaled deeply, grateful to be alive. He'd outwitted the savages, bested them at their own game, and lived to tell the tale. And what a story he would have for Shakespeare and his other friends! Appropriately embellished, of course, to make it more exciting than the experience had been. If that was possible.

Pegasus perked up immensely at the sight of the mountains. The gelding sensed that water and food were his as soon as he reached the beckoning vegetation, so up came his head and his stride lengthened appreciably.

Nate glanced over his shoulder. Cain and Smoky Woman were strolling arm in arm, Cain remarkably recovered for someone who had been at death's door. Flying Hawk, while still vigilant, was not as tense as before. All of them realized the worst of their ordeal was over.

Crossing the flat took about as long as he'd calculated. Seldom had simple grass and spruce trees looked so appealing as they did when he reached the bottom of a green slope and paused to inhale the fragrant spicy scent of the pines. Pegasus promptly lowered his muzzle and cropped greedily at the grass.

"Not yet," Nate said. "Just a little further."

A survey of the range showed he was north of the ravine through which Flying Hawk and he had passed to reach the wasteland. Was that the sole way in and out or was there another? He put the question to Cain.

"It's the only one I know of," Solomon answered, and nodded at the mountain towering above them. "Simon and me searched this here range for twenty miles or better from north to south, but we never did find another pass through to the other side."

"Then the ravine it is," Nate said, turning southward and pulling a reluctant Pegasus after him. Once through the ravine they would be in the park, and only there would he feel completely safe.

Doubts crept in as he walked along. He was assuming the savages seldom penetrated deep into the range, but what if he was wrong? Perhaps they did only roam the fringes of the mountains, which would explain why no one was aware of their existence. But maybe, just maybe, they wandered farther afield than he gave them credit for. In which case even the park wouldn't be a safe haven.

Enmeshed in mulling over what to do, Nate paid scant attention to his surroundings except when he scoured the land ahead for sign of the ravine. If he recalled correctly, it was situated snugly between a pair of peaks that effectively hid it until one was right on it.

Behind him Solomon Cain was talking. "You'll see, Smoky Woman. I ain't about to give up this easy. Once I'm well enough, I'll come back here and take out all the gold in that vein. The two of us will live in luxury for the rest of our lives."

"I no care for yellow rocks. I care for you."

"You're sweet. But if we're to live among white folks, we need the gold. You don't know how it is among my kind. Unless you have lots of money you're not considered worth much, and I'll be damned if I'm ever goin' to let any well-to-do folks look down their powdered noses at you."

"I be happy with just you," Smoky Woman stressed.

"Trust me. We need the gold."

"Is gold worth life?"

"I ain't about to die on you," Cain stated. "Not when I'm so close to havin' everything I've ever dreamed about, everything I could ever want. No, sirree."

Smoky Woman spoke so quietly Nate couldn't hear her words, but he did hear Cain's reply.

"Hell, no, woman. Don't be crazy. I ain't goin' to give up the gold for anything, not even you. If you love me you'll stick with me until this is all over and then the two of us will celebrate in St. Louis. Maybe we'll go on and do the same in New Orleans. The world will be ours." He paused and chuckled. "Why, we could even go to Paris, if we want. That's in Frenchy country."

"I see my people again?"

Nate could have counted to ten in the pregnant pause that greeted her query.

"Sure you will. I give you my word." Cain tittered. "And when you come back you'll have more foofaraw than all the women in your village put together. You'll be the talk of the tribe, the richest woman of them all."

"I just want you," Smoky Woman said plaintively.

Distracted by their conversation, Nate didn't recognize the opening to the ravine until he was directly abreast of it. Swinging around in surprise, he peered down its narrow length, jubilant at the thought that soon the wasteland would be a bitter memory and nothing more. Smiling, he beckoned the others and started into the ravine. Only now was he truly convinced they had eluded the savages. At long last they were really safe.

Suddenly a sharp cry of warning erupted from Flying Hawk's lips.

Spinning, Nate was horrified to see naked, hairy savages spilling from a wide crack he'd just passed in the left-hand wall, their intent signified by the feral gleams in their beady eyes and the lethal weapons poised in their brawny hands.

Chapter
Thirteen

So swiftly did the savages strike that they would have
been on Nate's party before anyone had a chance to
react if not for Flying Hawk. The Ute's eagle eyes
had registered motion in the crack a second before the
ferocious savages spilled forth, giving him time to yell
his warning and to snap his bow up. At such close range
deliberate aiming was unnecessary. He simply trained
his shaft on the chest of the foremost savage and released
the string.

The lead savage managed two more steps with a shaft
sticking from the center of his torso, then he collapsed
soundlessly, falling prone and causing the two Indians
behind him to stumble over his body. For a moment there
was a logjam at the opening as the ones who had tripped
regained their balance and those behind them slowed so
they wouldn't collide.

In that precious interval Nate leaped to the left, nearer
the crack, and jammed the Hawken to his shoulder.

161

He had to release the reins to shoot, and when he did Pegasus took off into the ravine, spurred by a screech from one of the fuming band.

Then, in the instant before Nate squeezed the trigger, time seemed to stand still. The thought flashed through his mind that he should have anticipated an ambush at the ravine since the ravine was the only way out of the wasteland on the east side. It wouldn't have taken a genius to figure out where they were headed and to send warriors on ahead to be waiting for them when they got there. The savages must have known all along. And now, like a rank greenhorn, Nate had walked right into their obvious trap.

The next moment Nate fired, sending a second savage into the hereafter. A third sprang at Smoky Woman, who stood temporarily paralyzed by shock. The savage's war club was poised to crush her skull, and would have done so the next moment if not for Cain, who leaped to her defense just as the club swooped down, putting himself between the Indian and her. Cain got an arm up in an effort to deflect the club, but in this he was only partially successful. The war club struck his forearm, glanced off, and smacked into the side of his head, dazing him. Before he could recover, the Indian swung again. This time the club caught him flush on the temple with a sickening thud.

Nate snatched a pistol out and took a hasty bead. The flintlock spat lead and smoke. Instantly the savage wielding the club sprouted a new eye.

Cain was on his knees, hands clasped to his head, blood pouring between his fingers. Smoky Woman, forgetting her own safety, leaned over at his side.

Another savage leaped toward her, this man armed with a spear. He would have impaled her if not for her brother, who streaked a glittering arrow into the man's soft throat.

162

Four enemies had been slain in the opening moments of the clash, yet more were spilling from the crack. Two more. Four. Five. And that was all, but it was more than enough.

Nate let the pistol he had just used fall from his fingers and grabbed at the other one, his hand closing on it just as a sneering savage charged and tried to smash his face in with a huge club. Hurling himself backwards saved him, but it also left him off balance, which the savage exploited by swinging at his midsection. The club grazed him, not doing much harm but acting much as would a shove by another person and sending him onto his backside in the dirt. His Hawken was jarred from his grip.

He began to scramble up and the club whistled at his skull. Throwing himself to the right, he rolled once. When he stopped, he held the flintlock. At the retort the savage's head whipped back, blood spurting from the man's mouth. Then the Indian staggered and fell.

Now the last of Nate's guns had been used, and as he was doing with increasing frequency of late, he relied on his tomahawk instead of his butcher knife. Jumping to his feet, he drew the tomahawk and spun. His heart, it felt like, leaped to his throat.

Two savages were grappling with Flying Hawk, the three men fighting tooth and nail. A third savage had Smoky Woman pinned and was trying to slit her throat. The last one was in the act of scalping Solomon Cain even though Cain was still alive, as demonstrated by his feeble resistance.

"No!" Nate roared. He was on the scalper before the Indian could rise, the tomahawk shearing the man's right eye in half and slicing off part of his face in the bargain.

Incensed, Nate spun again and attacked the savage on top of Smoky Woman. The savage saw him coming and shoved upright to meet his rush, but was unable to dodge the wicked swing that nearly took the Indian's head off.

Splattered with scores of red drops, Nate blinked and turned, intending to go to Flying Hawk's assistance. The pounding of feet gave him enough warning to brace himself, and then something struck him on his wounded shoulder and the world spun as he tottered rearward. Iron arms banded around his waist and he was borne to the ground. Knees gouged into his stomach.

Through a swirling haze he saw a grinning savage astride him, mouth curled in an expectant grin. He also saw the savage lift a war club. Urgently he tried to move his arms and legs, to buck the savage off, but his nerves refused to cooperate and send the proper signals from his brain to his limbs. All he did was twitch.

The savage, sensing his weakness, paused, perhaps to savor the moment. Then the club arced higher, bathed in the bright sunlight, and froze for a fraction of a second before beginning its downward plunge.

Nate stared eternity in the face and knew it. He gulped, strived to lift his arms. He saw a bestial light in his adversary's dark eyes. And then he saw something bulge out from between those eyes, a barbed point coated with crimson. The savage stiffened, gasped, and fell.

At last Nate felt he could move again, and he shoved the dead savage from him and rose. Not far off stood Flying Hawk, slowly lowering his bow. Closer were Smoky Woman and Cain, the latter flat on his back with a portion of his scalp hanging loose, the former in tears.

All of the savages were dead.

Or so they appeared as Nate surveyed the blood-soaked ground. Unwilling to leave anything to chance, he went from body to body, satisfying himself no spark of life remained in a single one. Then he joined the others in grim silence around Solomon Cain.

Suddenly Cain's eyes blinked open and his tongue touched his lips. "I reckon . . ." he said hoarsely, and stopped, grimacing in agony.

"Not talk," Smoky Woman chided, his hand cupped tenderly in hers.

Once more Cain's tongue moistened his lips. "Don't hardly matter, pretty one," he said. "I'm a gone beaver and I know it."

Nate almost replied, "No, you're not." But the side of Cain's head confirmed Cain's words. No man could live long with his brains oozing out. "Solomon, is there anything I can do for you?"

"Just do what you can for her," Cain said, his gaze flicking at the woman he loved.

"I will," Nate said, sounding as if he had a severe cold.

Flying Hawk added a string of words in Ute, then rested his hand on his sister's shoulder.

"Good," Cain said.

A nicker drew Nate's attention down the ravine where Pegasus was trotting back. When he next looked at Cain, Cain's eyes were closed. For a moment Nate thought the end at come, but he was premature.

"King?" Cain spoke in a strangled whisper.

"I'm here," Nate said.

"I have no kin to speak of, no one to mourn me when I'm gone. The gold is yours, all yours. Do what you want with it. I hope it brings you better luck than it brought me."

"I'm obliged," Nate responded, although he doubted he would ever be foolhardy enough to return to the cave. The savages were bound to keep an eye on it from now on. Perhaps—and here was a new thought that shocked him since it explained so much—perhaps the cave was a special place to the savages, a sacred site much as were the Paha Sapa hills to the Sioux and other areas to other tribes. If that was the case, any white man who set foot in the cave did so risking imminent death. All Indians were extremely protective of their sacred shrines, and every trapper who had lived with them for a while knew better than to violate a tribal sanctuary.

"You'll be rich," Cain was saying. "You can have anything you want."

Nate thought of his wife and son. "I already do."

"What?" Cain said. "You have gold already?"

"No," Nate said, and would have elaborated had not Cain erupted in a violent spasm of coughing and wheezing. The end was very near.

Smoky Woman threw herself on Cain's chest and unleased a torrent.

"I wish . . ." Cain cried, wild eyes fixed on the vast blue sky. "I wish . . ." But what he wished no one would ever know, for Solomon Cain's alloted time had run out. A gurgling whine escaped his lips. Then he went as rigid as a board, sucked in a great breath, and abruptly went totally limp.

Nate moved off to give Smoky Woman some privacy. Reclaiming his guns took a while, as did reloading them. When he led Pegasus over, she was standing in her brother's arms, but they self-consciously separated and took a step apart. "I'm sorry, Smoky Woman," he commented. "I truly am."

Too choked with emotion to speak, she merely nodded.

"We'll bury him, as is the custom with my people, and be on our way," Nate proposed. He nudged one of the savages with his toe. "There might be more of these Root Eaters or whatever they're called in the area, and we don't want to tangle with them again if we can help it."

"Where bury?" Smoky Woman asked.

The bottom of the ravine was hard, packed earth and rock. Without shovels and picks, digging a hole large enough to hold a man would take many hours. Maybe a full day. "How about near the spring yonder," Nate said, pointing toward the east opening.

Smoky Woman brightened slightly. "Yes. Please. That be nice."

They were a downcast lot as they trudged along, Nate with a hand on Cain to keep the corpse from sliding off Pegasus. The fight had added to his injuries and increased his fatigue, so when a patch of lush green grass appeared he barely checked a shout of unadulterated joy.

Before the burial each of them drank their full. Pegasus was still drinking when Nate located a suitable soft spot north of the spring and set to work with the tapered end of a stout branch. Flying Hawk watched him for a while, then joined in. Their corded muscles rippling, they excavated a suitable hole in less than an hour.

Nate stood on the lip and mopped sweat from his forehead. He could see a few thick worms wriggling at the bottom of the hole and he wished they had a buffalo robe or something else to wrap Cain in. But they didn't, so they would have to make do.

At a gesture from him, Flying Hawk grasped Cain's ankles. In unison they slowly lowered the body down on top of the worms. Nate began filling in the hole, working swiftly, oddly bothered by Cain's blank stare. Pausing, he reached down and closed Cain's eyelids.

Smoky Woman stood as if sculpted from marble the whole time. Her features inscrutable, she made no remarks whatsoever. Only when the final handful of dirt was cast down did she utter a soft, fluttering sigh.

"Do you care to say a few words?" Nate asked her.

"I not understand."

167

"Among my people it's customary to say a few nice things about those who have departed," Nate clarified. "It's our way of commending our souls to the spirit world."

"You say them."

"Me?" Nate blurted out, and repressed a frown. He was no minister. And while he must have read all of the Bible at one time or another, thanks to the influence of his mother and his required weekly church attendance, he wasn't exactly sure which words were appropriate for a funeral service. Not knowing what else to do, he recited the one passage in Scripture he knew by heart, the very first he had ever learned. "The Lord is my shepherd, I shall not want. He maketh me to lie down in green pastures; he leadeth me beside the still waters. He restoreth my soul: he leadeth me in the paths of righteousness for his name's sake. Yea, though I walk through the valley of the shadow of death, I will fear no evil; for thou art with me; thy rod and thy staff they comfort me." He stopped, unable to recall the rest. Then it came to him, haltingly. "Thou preparest a table before me in the presence of mine enemies: thou anointest my head with oil; my cup runneth over. Surely goodness and mercy shall follow me all the days of my life: and I will dwell in the house of the Lord for ever."

Smoky Woman stood with her head bowed in sorrow. Her brother had his arms folded across his chest, listening inquisitively.

"I reckon that's about it," Nate concluded. "Except maybe I should say that here was a man no better than most, no worse than many. I'm not fit to be his judge. But I was an accountant once, and I'd say his ledger came out on the plus side there at the end. For what it's worth."

Feeling uncomfortable, Nate donned his hat and walked to the spring. "I suppose we should rest up here

168

a day or two, then go find your village," he commented without looking around. "That is, if you want to live with your people, Smoky Woman. I know how rough it's going to be rearing your child among your tribe. Maybe you don't want to. Whatever you decide, I'll help out the best I can. I gave my word to Solomon." He paused. "What do you want to do, anyway?"

There was no answer.

Nate turned, and was flabbergasted to see Smoky Woman and Flying Hawk hiking southward. "Wait!" he found his voice. "Where are you going?"

She glanced back. "My brother find village where we maybe live. Where we be happy." Her smile warmed the very air. "Good-bye, Grizzly Killer. We never forget you."

"But . . ." Nate began, and stopped, knowing his words would be wasted. For the longest while he just stood there, watching the two figures grow smaller and smaller bit by bit, until eventually they faded into the forest and were gone from his life forever.

Bright and early the next morning he turned the Palouse homeward, humming as he rode.

WILDERNESS

By David Thompson

Tough mountain men, proud Indians, and an America that was wild and free—authentic frontier adventure set in America's black powder days.

#12: Apache Blood. When Nate and his family travel to the southern Rockies, bloodthirsty Apache warriors kidnap his wife and son. With the help of his friend Shakespeare McNair, Nate will save his loved ones—or pay the ultimate price.

__3374-7 $3.50 US/$4.50 CAN

#13: Mountain Manhunt. When Nate frees Solomon Cain from an Indian death trap, the apparently innocent man repays Nate's kindness by leaving him stranded in the wilds. Only with the help of a Ute brave can Nate set right the mistake he has made.

__3396-8 $3.50 US/$4.50 CAN

#14: Tenderfoot. To protect their families, Nate King and other settlers have taught their sons the skills that will help them survive. But young Zach King is still a tenderfoot when vicious Indians capture his father. If Zach hasn't learned his lessons well, Nate's only hope will be a quick death.

__3422-0 $3.50 US/$4.50 CAN